For more than forty years,
Yearling has been the leading name
in classic and award-winning literature
for young readers.

Yearling books feature children's
favorite authors and characters,
providing dynamic stories of adventure,
humor, history, mystery, and fantasy.

Trust Yearling paperbacks to entertain,
inspire, and promote the love of reading
in all children.

the friskative dog

susan straight

A YEARLING BOOK

Published by Yearling, an imprint of Random House Children's Books
a division of Random House, Inc., New York

Yearling and the jumping horse design are registered trademarks of Random House, Inc.

Visit us on the Web! www.randomhouse.com/kids

Educators and librarians, for a variety of teaching tools, visit us at www.randomhouse.com/teachers

The Library of Congress has cataloged the hardcover edition of this work as follows:
Straight, Susan.
The Friskative Dog / Susan Straight.
p. cm.
Summary: Sharron's father has disappeared, and she tries to cope with her feelings of
loss through the love of a stuffed dog he gave her.
ISBN: 978-0-375-83777-7 (trade) — ISBN: 978-0-375-93777-4 (lib. bdg.)
[1. Loss (Psychology)—Fiction. 2. Missing persons—Fiction. 3. Dogs—Fiction.
4. Toys—Fiction. 5. Fathers—Fiction. 6. Schools—Fiction.] I. Title.
PZ7.S8955Fr 2007
[Fic]—dc22
2006016074

ISBN: 978-0-440-42145-0 (pbk.)

Reprinted by arrangement with Alfred A. Knopf Books for Young Readers

Printed in the United States of America

August 2008

10 9 8 7 6 5 4 3 2 1

First Yearling Edition

This book is dedicated to Rosette and Teddy, and
Celeste and Fannie, and the listening faces
of Mrs. Melton's fourth-grade class, whose ears
and opinions were immensely helpful,
as was Mrs. Melton.

the friskative dog

One

Sharron couldn't sleep at night without The Friskative Dog. When she rubbed her fingers along the fur on his shoulders, sparks shone in the darkness of her bedroom, like he made his own little stars.

Now she sat with her spine against her bedroom wall, dog at her side, doing her homework. Her mother's voice rolled along gentle and ripply and gold like water at the curb. She talked on the phone every night in her bedroom. Through the wall, Sharron couldn't hear the words. Just the murmuring, like fingertips tracing the paint at her back.

Fourth-grade math was hard. It was November

1

and the class was doing algebra. X stood for something you had to find out. X factor was the mystery.

Her mother always said, "Look, sweetie, I can't help you with that math. I put the items over the magic window, and the register tells me the numbers. I just take the money and smile. I'm not the one good with math. Your father was."

Her father was gone. He had disappeared a year ago, but still her mother talked about him at night. Sharron could tell. No laughing or joking. Her mother talked to Aunt Dickie, her sister who had moved to Germany with her husband, who was in the army. Her mother talked to her best friend, Leila, who worked with her at the market. And once a week, on Thursday nights when they were planning what to make for dinner the next night, she talked to Grandma Pat. Daddy's mother.

Those nights, her voice was light and cheerful, and Sharron knew her mother was trying to make Grandma Pat understand that they were fine, they were waiting, they were patient.

"Have patience," Grandma Pat said every Friday, when she came over for dinner. "They'll find him. He got hit on the head. He doesn't know where he is."

Grandma Pat's hair was always in a bun, sitting like an unbaked biscuit on her head. Cut out and round and white. Every Friday, at six-ten, she always said the same thing.

She thought he'd gotten into an accident somewhere and he had the memory disease.

"He's got insomnia," Grandma Pat said. She put down enchilada casserole on the table. The casserole dish had a lid always covered with steam like fog.

Sharron said, "That means he can't sleep at night. You mean amnesia."

"That's the one," Grandma Pat said. "When his memory comes back, he'll come back. He'll find his way." She patted Sharron's mother on the shoulder.

That night, Sharron sat with her back against the wall so she could feel her mother's low voice. When his memory comes back. What if it didn't? People didn't know their way home like dogs did.

People couldn't just walk across the country, like in one of her favorite books, *The Incredible Journey.* A man couldn't sleep in a field at night, catch a rabbit to eat, hide in a barn, and swim across a river and then walk into his apartment a year later.

Dogs had something inside their brains. A locator. A tracker. At school, Piper said her mother's new car had GPS. A voice that talked to the driver from the dashboard and told her mother where to go. Global Positioning System.

People didn't have anything like that inside them.

She rubbed the softness of her dog's ears. Dogs that accidentally got taken all the way across the state somehow found their way home. They trotted through fields and crossed streams and highways, and they showed up in their own yards dirty and tired, and still their tongues hung out when they saw their people.

They don't have amnesia, because they love their people. Maybe my father does have insomnia, too, Sharron thought. Like me. She lay down on her bed, her back still against the wall. Her mother's voice had stopped. I have insomnia. That's why I need The Friskative Dog.

Her father had bought him, but her mother claimed he'd liked the rabbit better.

Her father used to say, "No, I saw this guy and knew he was the one. Those cute little ears." Her mother used to smile and shake her head. "You wanted to get the rabbit, but I said this guy was perfect for Sharron for Christmas. She was only five, but she knew all the different kinds of dogs. Remember? Cocker spaniels and dachshunds and Dobermans. I saw this yellow Labrador retriever puppy, and I knew she had to have him. I remember how soft his fur felt."

Her mother liked to tease Sharron about how she made up her own names for things back when she was three and four. Her mother would say, "I'll never forget one day, out in the yard, we saw a huge

5

bee on the bottlebrush tree, and you said, 'Look at that bumblebee's antlers!'

"Early in the morning, before the sun was up," she would say sometimes, even now that Sharron was nine, "you'd hear that rumbling noise and you'd say, 'Here comes the streetcreeper.'

"And at night, I'd be sitting with you on your bed, and we'd hear a siren, and you'd say, 'Listen— the ambulamp is coming. Watch for the red light on the wall!' "

And when her father bought her the puppy and he'd danced across the floor, Sharron said, "This doggie is so friskative!"

She remembered saying that word. She didn't need anyone to remind her.

Those were words Grandma Pat used to say about Sharron. "Look at this little girl," her grandmother would laugh. "Just as frisky and playful as can be. And so talkative."

Sharron's puppy never barked. He just leapt and moved and scrambled across her bedspread while she held the leash. She kept the leash on him even when they slept. She never wanted him to run away. Every night, back then when she was small, while she lay with her dog under the covers, she had touched his hard, cold eyes to make them warm and soft with her own fingers.

Two

●●●●●●●●

She had taken him to school once each year. Carried him across the playground of Emily Dickinson Elementary.

In first grade, the teacher, Mrs. G, said they could bring in pets for show-and-tell.

Juan-Carlos brought an iguana in an aquarium. The iguana had green skin and a little fringe that stood up along his neck, like a thin lizard Mohawk. He said his mother hated the iguana. He fed it crickets and lettuce and fruit. The iguana's name was Butch.

Eboni brought a rabbit. The rabbit was black-and-white-spotted, with whiskers that shivered. Her name was Freckles. Eboni said Freckles ate carrots and alfalfa. Freckles stomped her feet when the class crowded around. That meant she was scared.

Piper brought a big dog with reddish gold fur, like a sunset. "My dog's name is Carlotta," she said proudly. "She's a golden retriever with papers. She cost eight hundred dollars. She eats special food to keep her fur pretty, and I brush her every day."

She showed the class the special brush and the dog biscuits she gave for a treat. Everyone held out their hands to pet Carlotta.

On Friday, Sharron brought The Friskative Dog. She hadn't said anything to her mother about show-and-tell. She put The Friskative Dog in her backpack but left the top unzipped so he could breathe. When she walked across the playground, his nose poked out and kids ran across the grass, screaming, "That girl's got a dog in there! Look! He's trying to get out!"

The big kids reached behind Sharron to grab The Friskative Dog, and she ran all the way to her classroom.

When they sat on the floor for show-and-tell, Sharron carried him into the center of the circle and held him with his thin purple leash. She had brought his plate. The night before, she had taken a plain white dinner plate from the cupboard when her mother wasn't looking, and she'd painted her dog's initials in purple nail polish.

TFD. She didn't know how to spell his name. They hadn't learned how to write big words yet. She could write The and Dog. But she knew Friskative began with F.

Piper laughed out loud first and pointed at Sharron and her dog. "That's not a real dog!" she shouted. "That's just a stuffed animal."

"He's a yellow Lab puppy," Sharron said loudly. "He has papers. He cost a lot of money. My dad bought him for me at Christmas last year. His name is The Friskative Dog because he's always leaping around on my bed."

She pulled the leash and he leapt into the air. She let him land gently on the carpet.

"He's not even a Beanie Baby," Piper said.

"He's the size of a dog," Sharron said. "Beanie Babies are little."

"He's not a real dog," Juan-Carlos said.

"He sleeps with me every night."

Mrs. G said, "Let's write down Sharron's dog's name on the blackboard next to the names of our other pets this week."

"The Friskative Dog," Sharron said again.

Mrs. G didn't even have to ask how to spell it. She wrote in careful perfect letters. K. There was a K. And a V.

"That's not even a word," Piper said, her mouth mean and downturned like a crescent roll.

Sharron said, "Yes, it is. You just haven't learned it yet."

Eboni raised her hand, the way the children were supposed to when they sat in a circle.

"Yes, Eboni?" Mrs. G said.

"What does your dog eat?" Eboni asked. That was what they always asked about pets.

Sharron smiled at Eboni. Eboni smiled back. "My dog eats exactly what I eat."

"My mom says it's not good for dogs to eat people food," Piper whispered loudly.

"My mom says whatever's good enough for me is good enough for The Friskative Dog," Sharron said. She petted his ears. They were soft and warm from her arms. "He eats Lucky Charms in the morning. Seven. And he eats peanut butter crackers while I'm gone to school. One. And at dinner, he eats whatever we eat. Hot dogs. Bacon. Sometimes rice."

"We eat mangoes," Juan-Carlos said. "Sometimes I give a piece to Butch."

"Where does he poop, then?" Piper shouted.

"I didn't see you raise your hand," Mrs. G said, folding her arms, and Piper stuck her hand up in the air. She had on three rings.

Sharron said, "My mom says that's why he's the best dog in the world, because she doesn't have to clean up after him. He sleeps in my bed every night."

"Dogs are supposed to sleep in doghouses," Piper said.

"Iguanas don't sleep at night. They walk around," Juan-Carlos said.

"What does your dog like to eat best?" Eboni said.

"He likes to eat love."

"Love!" they all said.

"I kiss him on his mouth and he calls it love." Sharron felt her dog's paws move on her arm. Everyone in the circle stared at her. Now she was finished. The other kids had parents who came and took their pets home. Sharron carried her dog to her cubbyhole and let him sit facing out, so he could watch her while she sat back at her desk.

In second grade, Mrs. R read the class a book called *The Velveteen Rabbit*.

The rabbit was a stuffed toy, but the little boy who owned him loved him so much that The Velveteen Rabbit turned real. Real meant love. Sharron stared at the pictures again and again. The little rab-bit sat in the grass with the other rabbits. Real rabbits. The Velveteen Rabbit had stitches on its back. But when the little boy was very sick, and the rabbit was taken outside to be thrown away, he turned real.

In second grade, there was no show-and-tell. Everyone waited until their Day as a Star.

Each student got to be Star. You made a poster about your life and your house and your parents and your pets. You brought your parents if they could come, right after lunch, and your pet, if you wanted to, and you read one sentence from your favorite book.

Piper's poster was the size of a mattress. She had two little brothers, both blond like her, their eyes blue as swimming pools. They had a swimming pool. She had so many pictures: Piper on her swimming-pool slide; Piper with her dog, Carlotta, in the big backyard with flowers and a wooden fort; and Piper in her room with a flowery bedspread and her own TV.

She brought her mother and father and her little brothers in their stroller. Her father held the leash for Carlotta. Piper brought the book *Mulan*, but there was no time to read a sentence, because her little brothers started to cry.

Eboni's poster showed her and her mother in front of their house, with shingles and a porch like in "Hansel and Gretel." Eboni's mother had braids like Eboni, and they wore the same outfit—black leggings and pink shirts with hearts and their names painted on. Eboni's mother was a nurse. She wore a white uniform in one picture. Eboni's rabbit had a huge cage in their backyard, with a water bowl and carrots and her own bushes.

Eboni's mother came in her white nurse uniform. She said she was on lunch break from the hospital. She brought a stethoscope for everyone to listen to their own heart. Sharron's heart sounded like wind in the round circles at her ears. Eboni had brought her rabbit, Freckles, who thumped in her cage again. Eboni's favorite book was *Moosetache*. She read:

*"He could barely bop and hip-hop with a moose-
tache going flip-flop."*

Sharron's mother helped her make a poster. It
had a picture of her father driving his truck that said
SWIFT. He wore a red baseball cap, and his elbow
hung over the door. Sharron loved how loud and
trembly that truck could be. Her father kept it
parked down the street in the empty lot, because at
the apartment where they lived, the carport was very
small.

Her mother had brought home a disposable cam-
era from the store where she worked. They took pictures of the flower bed and palm trees around the
sign in front of the apartments that said *Palm Gardens*. They took a picture of the pool. They took a
picture of Sharron sitting in her father's lap, holding
her hands on the big steering wheel of his truck. Her
father's shirt smelled of pancakes and syrup, but his
hands smelled of tires.

They took a picture of Sharron sitting on her bed with The Friskative Dog.

They decorated the poster with purple stars from the store, and Sharron drew flowers and bones and hearts with purple marker.

She brought The Friskative Dog for her Day as a Star, with his purple leash. He sat on her desk all day.

Her mother couldn't come at lunch, because that was a busy time at the market. And her father was driving his truck to Georgia for three days. He was carrying big recliner chairs to Atlanta.

Sharron stood up after lunch in front of the class to be Star. She said, "My dad drives a big truck. He buys me something from each state, a little license plate magnet." She held up Pennsylvania. "My mom keeps them on the refrigerator."

"Is that your pool?" Juan-Carlos said, pointing at the poster.

"That's an apartment pool. There's a lifeguard sign," Piper said.

Sharron said, "I swim there every day in the summer. And The Friskative Dog swims with me."

"He can't swim," Piper said.

"Your dog isn't allowed in the pool," Sharron said. "Your mom told us. But my dog loves to swim. He floats right next to me."

She held him close to her chest. "This is my dog. He's real. I loved him so much he turned real when I was five. He listens to me every night. I can see his eyes move. And sometimes I wake up and he's underneath my neck. He moved there."

"You probably grab him when you're sleeping," Piper said, rolling her eyes. "He's a stuffed animal."

"I wonder what they stuff animals with," Juan-Carlos said.

"In the book, the rabbit was real because his boy loved him," Eboni said. "You have to believe."

From her favorite book, *The Velveteen Rabbit*, Sharron read:

"Does it hurt?" asked the Rabbit. "Sometimes,"
said the Skin Horse, for he was always truthful.
"When you are Real you don't mind being hurt."

"That was three sentences," Piper said.

Mrs. R said, "We were just going to read one, Sharron."

"But Piper didn't read at all, so I was using her sentence," Sharron said, and she smiled.

Sharron sat back down with her poster taped to her desk and her dog in her lap.

Her father always said, first thing when he came home from a long truck-driving trip, "How's that doggie? Getting in any trouble? I hope not, 'cause he sure is cute sitting there on the couch with you. Were you looking out the window for me?"

"We were!" Sharron used to shout. "Mama said you were coming home Tuesday, and today is Tuesday!"

Her father used to pat her dog on the head and

say, "What a good puppy!" Then he'd pick Sharron up and put her on his shoulders, and he would gallop like a horse down to the truck, where she would find her magnet from Alabama or Florida or New Mexico.

In third grade, each class had a pet parade. Everyone brought their pets and walked through the auditorium, showing their pets to the kindergarten and first-grade classes at an assembly. Piper's dog barked at Eboni's rabbit. Juan-Carlos held his iguana's cage, and Brittany carried her goldfish in a bowl while the water swayed and the fish stayed still, staring at the air with big black eyes.

Sharron led The Friskative Dog on his leash just after Brittany. He scooted along the hard floor of the cafeteria, and the little kids pointed and laughed. But Sharron smiled. Her dog was better than a goldfish or a lizard. You couldn't sleep with a fish, and you couldn't kiss an iguana.

Her father had driven his truck to Atlanta again that fall, when Sharron was eight. He'd said, "I have only short runs in October. San Francisco, Stockton, Fresno." He drove loads of recliner chairs all over California just before Halloween. Sharron and her mother put jack-o'-lanterns on the balcony of the apartment, and in the big front window that looked over the courtyard and the pool, Sharron hung the scarecrow and witch she'd made in first and second grades.

She asked her mother if they could buy a plain white dish towel at the market. It was $1.79. Sharron cut two eyeholes in the dish towel and made a black mouth with a marker. She put the ghost costume on The Friskative Dog. In her mother's closet, she had seen a prom dress from when her parents were in high school. Her mother said Sharron could wear it.

She and The Friskative Dog trick-or-treated all

around Palm Gardens Apartments. Other kids were on the balconies, too, going from door to door and then down the cement steps around the pool. Sharron saw Brittany, who lived in the apartments across the street, and even Juan-Carlos, whose house was two blocks over.

"I like trick-or-treating at your place 'cause you don't have to walk so far to get a lot of candy," Juan-Carlos said. "Are you like a disco queen?"

Sharron said, "I'm prom queen. My dog is a ghost. And you're a pirate."

On November 4, her father said, "I have to take a long run to Atlanta again."

And he'd never come back.

He didn't answer his cell phone, even though Sharron's mother left fourteen messages. Then the cell-phone number was disconnected. Sharron's mother called the SWIFT trucking agency. They said he hadn't taken his truck, that there wasn't any scheduled run to Atlanta for a truckload of recliners going to a furniture store.

Sharron's mother called the police. The two men asked her mother so many questions that Sharron fell asleep while trying to listen through the bedroom door.

But it had been almost a year now, and no one had heard anything from her father.

Three

●●●●●●●●

Every day, Sharron walked home from school and passed the palm trees around the sign that read *Palm Gardens*. Yesterday it had been windy, and many palm fronds had fallen to the grass. Two of the younger kids, Manuel and Gracie, were galloping with the fronds between their legs, like they rode horses. Palm fronds looked just like horses, when you were small. The brown collar, the bent neck, and the long tail that ended with the brown threads at the tips of the fronds. You had to make sure all the thorns were worn off. Sharron used to ride the palm-frond horses when she was little.

She walked up the pebbled steps to the second floor. Last year, she used to sit on these steps and try to count the stones—gray gravel and white pebbles and brown rocks—in three of the steps to see if they were all exactly the same. But she couldn't keep track because there were no lines or squares.

But I could estimate, she realized today. I could count the stones in one section and mark it off and figure out how many to multiply by. She grabbed The Friskative Dog and some paper and a pencil and sat on the top step.

In one square, there were forty-two stones. There would be ten squares in the whole step.

That meant 420 stones in each large step. And there were ten steps. That meant 4,200 stones!

Piper has never counted anything this big, Sharron thought. I know it. Piper can count her Barbies and her shoes and her DVDs. But even all together, it wouldn't come close to 4,200.

She studied The Friskative Dog's paws. They were dirty from his running around on the stairway and the walkway outside the apartment door.

"You need a bath," she told him.

When she was little, learning to swim in the pool below, she really had taken him into the water with her. He bobbed and floated and stayed right beside her. But then he had to be dried. He sat outside on a towel in the sun for an hour or so, and his fur got hard and stiff from the chlorine in the pool, her mother said.

So Sharron made her mother take her to the pet section at the market. Leashes and collars and dog shampoo and brushes. Her mother bought one of each, and that's why The Friskative Dog wore a purple collar, had a small purple leash, and smelled good.

She sat on the couch with The Friskative Dog. She watched the kids riding around the pool fence and the flower beds, and she watched the other doors across the second floor. All the doors were light green, the color of mint ice cream. On her door, the metal number said 14. From the front window, she could see 17, 18, and 19.

Manuel and Gracie's mother had a bird. A blue parakeet. He sat in his cage in the front window, and Sharron could hear him chirp like an alarm clock. Even though Mrs. Hernandez kept the door closed so the bird wouldn't bother the other people, you could hear him talking to her.

Sharron's mother came up past the kids and waved. She carried one bag of groceries from the market, like every day.

"You didn't come to the store so we could walk home together," she said when Sharron met her at the stairs.

"I wanted to start my homework."

"I still don't like you being alone."

"I'm nine now. I'm only alone from three until three-thirty if you come home."

Sharron's mother stopped sorting out the ba-nanas and the Rice Krispies on the table. "*If* I come home?"

Sharron shrugged. She didn't know why she'd

said it. This was the first week she'd told her mother she didn't want to walk from school to the market and wait for her. She didn't feel like doing her homework on the bench in front of the store. She didn't feel like talking to the other checkers and the baggers. She wanted to start her reading and be alone after school. She wanted to sit on the couch with The Friskative Dog and think for a while.

"*If?*" Sharron's mother said again, and she came over to the couch. She held out a fruit roll for Sharron. "I will always come home. Every single day. At three-thirty. But it's hard for me not to see you at the store."

Her mother's eyes were gray, shiny gray like eucalyptus leaves with their silvery shimmer. Sharron's own eyes were brown like her father's, dark as gingerbread. Her father used to say, "Hey, gingerbread eyes!"

Sharron looked out the window. She didn't want to see her mother's eyes even shinier with tears. "I have a big project from school," she said. "It's due the week before Christmas vacation. We're doing reports on what we want to be. Career reports."

Her mother leaned her head back on the couch and took off her shoes. "What do you want to be? You used to say nurse, teacher, or vet. Looks like as much as you love dogs, you should be a vet."

Sharron picked up The Friskative Dog with her left hand and her schoolbooks with her right. "I don't know," she said. "I have to do a lot of reading to decide." Then she went into her room.

She had checked out extra books from the library. Her teacher, Mrs. Monson, had given her a note for the librarian. She laid out the books on her bed and ate the apricot fruit roll while she read.

Everyone said, "If you love animals, you should be a vet." But Sharron had read about veterinarians. They were doctors for animals. They gave dogs and cats shots, they checked their eyes and ears and bodies, they set broken legs, and sometimes they put dogs or other animals to sleep.

She closed the book. She didn't want to watch a

dog close his eyes. She didn't want to watch anyone cry. She didn't want to hold a needle.

"Well, there are other careers that might revolve around dogs," Mrs. Monson said when they discussed jobs in class. They were making schedules for when to present their reports. It would be next month, in December. Right now they were still choosing careers and finding pictures in magazines.

Piper said she wanted to stay home and raise kids, like her mom. Juan-Carlos wanted to be a firefighter, like his dad. Eboni wanted to be a nurse, like her mom. Brittany wanted to be a hairdresser, like her grandmother. Ray didn't want to be a coach like his dad; he wanted to be a star in the NBA. Patrick didn't want to be a roofer like his dad, because he said it was too hot in the summer. He wanted to be a policeman.

I don't want to work at La Reina Market like my mom, Sharron thought. She said, "I'm still deciding."

Piper said, "Maybe you can make stuffed animals," and she grinned like she thought she was so smart.

Sharron said, "Maybe you can buy my animals for your kids. Maybe I'll sell them for a hundred dollars."

She went outside for recess. Her mother always told her, "Don't let Piper think she's better than you. She's got more money. But you've got more brains."

Sharron sat on her bed all night and read the books she'd brought home. Her favorite was *Dog Breeds of the World*.

There were pictures and paragraphs about each kind of dog. Dalmatians. Labrador retrievers. Irish setters. Russian wolfhounds. Even Egyptian hairless dogs.

Dogs had come from all over the world. They swam across streams, they padded over sand, they hunted in the woods. They sat on ladies' laps—the Pomeranians—with bows at their ears, and their job was to love an old woman. They brought bread and whiskey to people trapped in the snow—the Saint Bernards. They lived in the firehouses—the dalmatians. They carried ducks in their mouths—the English pointers—and dropped them at their masters' boots. Sharron loved the border collies from Scotland—their job was to herd sheep, all day, running in circles around the sheep and making them move to different fields.

She got up to get a dish of ice cream when the apartment was very dark, and she heard her mother on the phone with Leila. She didn't know how her mother could work at the market all day with Leila and then have more to talk to her about at night. Her mother was saying, "I know I need a car. Every day I see that carport empty and I think Sharron is going to need me to take her to the mall when she gets older. She's going to have to ride the bus to junior high. But I have to pick one thing to save for, and I need the big thing more. I have to be patient."

Sharron didn't know what Leila said, but her

mother laughed. "Yeah, like his mother, Pat, says every week. Be patient. Do you know today is November fourth? It's been exactly a year since he took off."

Whatever Leila said, Sharron's mother didn't laugh this time. She said, "Sharron's patient, too. Very patient. It's up to me now to make sure she has what she needs, and she's going to be so happy when we get this. Someday."

Sharron stood in the kitchen. She couldn't move. The cold air came out from the freezer. Her mother hung up and went out to the balcony to water the ivy plant that hung from the wrought-iron railing.

What was her mother saving for? A dog? A dog couldn't be something bigger than a car, something that required more money than could be saved in a year.

Back in her room, Sharron started to fall asleep with the books on the floor beside her bed. She could hear her mother's voice in the next room and knew she must be talking to Grandma Pat. Her mother's voice was cheerful. She said, "Tomorrow's Friday. We can talk about it then."

Sharron held The Friskative Dog close under her chin. She said, "Your job is to stay warm, and help me think, and keep me company. Forever."

Four

●●●●●●●

She didn't want him to become real.

She woke up in the middle of the night and went out to sit on the couch in the dark. She held The Friskative Dog tightly. The pool shimmered and made watery moons on the doors across the court-yard. Sharron looked out onto the street. Once she had seen a coyote run down the middle of the street, his feet on the painted white lines like they were his path through the darkness. His tail was long and held low, like a thin palm frond. He was huge. It was summer, hot all night, and Sharron's window was open. She'd heard sirens and cars, and something had called her to the window. She watched the coy-ote move swiftly up to the fence surrounding the pool. He'd pushed his nose against the gate and then turned and run out of the courtyard and back down the street.

Mrs. Hernandez had said, "Oh, *los coyotes*! They are dangerous!"

Sharron's mother had said, "They eat cats and even small dogs. I heard that from a customer at the store. She lost her Chihuahua to a coyote one summer."

Sharron stared out the window now. She'd awakened crying. Her dog was wet from her tears. She had dreamed of the coyote, and a truck on the highway, and a barbed-wire fence all along the road.

If The Friskative Dog turned real, he would have to go outside someday. Like The Velveteen Rabbit, he would leave. He would run to the river bottom where the coyotes lived. To the hills around the city. She held him close. His fur smelled of her coconut shampoo.

She put her chin on the arm of the couch and

watched the pool. All her life, she had seen this water out this window. She had seen wasps hover over the pool and drink, and swallows whose nests were under the eaves of the apartment building, even butterflies sometimes in summer. They thought this was a pond, in a meadow, like in the books.

One night her father had been awake and watching with her. She had a fever. She was small. She lay on the backrest of the couch, high up on the narrow pillows, trying to feel the air because she was so hot, and the windows were open, and her father held her up there with his hand. "Cool you off," he'd said. He turned on the fan, and the wind blew over her. She watched the blue pool water move, and her father had said, "A little breeze off the lake down there. Cool you off." Then he'd said, "Sharron, look at that, look at those babies."

A possum had slipped through the fence bars and was walking near the pool. On her back rode lumps of baby. Baby possums. "I count seven," her father had said, near her ear. "Look at the mama drinking from that puddle near the shallow end, where all your friends splashed out that water."

Sharron laid her head on the couch now and cried. A year. What if she never saw her father again? What if he'd been kidnapped on his way to his truck? Why hadn't the police ever come back?

She had never seen the coyote again. She held her dog tightly, got up from the couch, and pushed her way back under the covers of her bed.

In class, Mrs. Monson said, "Have you noticed that many girls choose their mothers' careers, and many boys choose the jobs their fathers do? What do you think of that?"

The students were quiet for a moment. "My dad says when you're a coach, people are only happy when you win," Ray said. "They're mad at you if your team loses."

Mrs. Monson said, "But if you're an NBA star, people will expect you to win all the time, too."

Ray pretended to shoot a basket and said, "But I'll have lots of money, and my dad says coaching high school is never going to make him rich."

Mrs. Monson laughed. She said, "Does anyone in here think about doing the job of the other parent in your family? Or the grandparent?"

Sharron looked down at her desk. All the thin lines of the wood grain were like rain blowing sideways across her father's windshield; she'd driven around the block with him several times. But she'd never even been able to go on a short haul; it was too dangerous, her father said, and he had to unload heavy crates or boxes or chairs.

She didn't want to be a truck driver, to drive all day down the freeways and highways and streets, leave something for someone, and turn around to do the whole thing again.

Her father used to say, "I had to fight my way to San Francisco and fight my way back. So many cars." But she knew he loved the highway.

Eboni said, "My father died."

"I'm sorry, Eboni," Mrs. Monson said.

"He was an X-ray man at the hospital. He met my mom there. But his heart stopped working." She wiped her eyes. "I don't want to be the X-ray person, because what if that wasn't good for his heart?"

Sharron said, "If you're a nurse, you could work with your mom and eat lunch together."

Mrs. Monson said, "Being a nurse is hard, too. Sometimes patients are in pain or crying." She looked around the room. "I like what Sharron's been doing about her career project. She's been reading books about jobs. I'd like everyone to check out a library book about the career they're thinking of. It will help you know the real details of the job. The good parts and the hard parts."

Piper raised her hand and waved it back and forth like a fan. "My mom says the most important job in the world is to stay home and raise her children."

Mrs. Monson smiled. "Yes, I've heard her say that. She's told me many times. But it's also good to do other things, if someone wants to. My twins are over in the kindergarten classroom right now, and Mrs. B is teaching them while I'm teaching you."

"Well," Piper said, "my mom says she gets her instructions from her heart and from God."

Mrs. Monson said, "That's fine. But you still need to check out a book. Maybe a book on parenting."

At home, Sharron sat on the stairs with The Friskative Dog. On the sidewalk, Mrs. Gutierrez walked past with her German shepherd. She walked him twice a day. She waved at Sharron. Then, just as Sharron's mother came into the courtyard, Sharron saw Mr. Hartley. He had four dogs on leashes today—two poodles, a Yorkshire terrier, and a beagle. Mr. Hartley was a dog walker.

After dinner, Sharron looked out the window at the sidewalk and the balconies and the pool. Being a dog walker meant you'd have to pick up poop all day and then take the dogs back to their owners. That didn't sound like much fun. Being a dog groomer meant you clipped and shaved and washed, and dogs probably hated the blow-dryer. That sounded messy and hard.

Every Friday, Grandma Pat brought something for dinner. Something in the glass casserole dish. Lasagna. Macaroni-cheese-tuna. Enchiladas. She asked Sharron about school, and when Sharron told her about the career project, Grandma Pat said, "I grew up picking oranges in the groves with my parents. I always wanted to be a pilot, like Amelia Earhart. But my mother said, 'Look at how she crashed and they never found her. I couldn't stand that.' So my mother told me to become a secretary, and I did that until I retired."

"Did you like it?" Sharron asked, watching the steam rise around the spatula when her grandmother cut into the food.

Grandma Pat stopped and looked at her. Her glasses had twinkly rhinestones at the corners, and her hair was in the bun. "I wore a suit every day, and I answered the phone, and I typed letters, and at lunch I sat with my friends and we ate a piece of pie for dessert. We all worked in a big law firm downtown. We never went outside until the end of the day." She moved a plate closer to her. "I guess I liked knowing what would happen every day. But your father, he came to see me once and rode up to the eleventh floor in the elevator, and he said he'd never work inside like I did. He said he wanted to be a race-car driver."

"But when we got married, he said a truck driver always had work," Sharron's mother said. "And he always had a good job with SWIFT."

"He'll call us soon," Grandma Pat said, when they were all quiet for a time. "He'll figure it out. He'll remember who he is, and where he's supposed to be."

Five

━━━━━━━━

"**W**here are you supposed to be?"

The yard-duty teacher's voice scared Sharron. His name was Mr. Howard, and he said, "You can't sit here by the library. You're supposed to be on the playground for recess."

Sharron took her book and walked slowly back toward the playground, but she wouldn't go near the picnic benches, where she usually liked to read. A new girl had come to their fourth-grade class, a girl named Paige, and even though she'd only been at school for a week, she and Piper were best friends.

Piper and Paige kept coming up to Eboni and Sharron and Brittany wherever they were and telling them they had to move. At the big oak tree

44

where they collected acorns and pretended to be Indians, Piper said, "We already put dibs on the tree at lunch. You have to move. Paige is the new girl, and I'm showing her everything."

At the picnic benches, Piper said to Sharron, "It's recess. You're supposed to play games. Not read books about dogs when you don't even have one."

Paige said, "I heard you have a stuffed animal and you say he's real." Her hair was long and brown and in a perfect ponytail. That's why it was called a ponytail, Sharron realized, staring at Paige. Like a horse's tail. She could smell hair spray on the little curl at the end when Paige came close to her. "I have two turtles and a rottweiler. My dog protects our house. What does your dog protect?"

Piper smiled. "No one would break into your apartment, 'cause there's nothing to steal. You have, like, one room."

Sharron stood up. "We have four rooms."

Paige said, "We have four bedrooms in our house and four bathrooms."

Piper said, "We have five bedrooms and a pool."

"We have a pool, too," Sharron said, but even as the words came out from her teeth, she knew what Piper would say.

"Your pool is nasty," Piper shouted, and the other kids near the oak tree stopped to listen. "All the people in your apartments can swim there and pee."

Sharron looked up at the oak branches. She remembered what her father said when she used to tell him about Piper. "She's named for an airplane? A little tiny airplane? That's funny. Don't ever let some little plane buzz you and make you duck."

Sharron said, "Your little brothers pee in your pool. Rich pee isn't different. It's all invisible. You drink it every day."

Piper and Paige both let their mouths fall open, like the parakeet's when he saw food coming toward his cage. Then they ran off to the classroom.

When Sharron got to the door, Mrs. Monson was listening to the two girls, and the other kids were lining up because recess was over. Piper said loudly, "Sharron said I drink pee."

Sharron folded her arms. "Everyone drinks some pool water when they swim. That's what I said to her. Everyone's the same."

"No, they're not," Piper said.

Mrs. Monson held up her hands in the stop sign. "In my classroom, they are. Everybody, go in and sit down. And remember, all your chairs are exactly the same."

She didn't smile at Sharron, but she didn't frown, either.

That afternoon, instead of going straight home, Sharron walked to La Reina Market, where her mother worked. It was November 12, and the sky was dark and gray. The wind tossed the branches of the pepper tree at the corner.

She sat on the bench in front of the store and watched the customers come and go. Brown bags with things poking out the top: green ends of carrots like hair, long French bread like a sword, a spatula. One woman carried only a clear plastic bag filled with pink speckled pinto beans, like hundreds of pretty pebbles.

Sharron heard her mother's voice inside. Whenever the sliding doors opened, her mother was saying, "I can't believe you cut your hair so short" or "Look at how tall he's gotten all of a sudden!"

Her mother's voice wasn't a ripply stripe of gold at Sharron's back. It was a silvery shifting of palm fronds, constant and breezy—her voice for the market, not for home.

She was thinking about Piper and Paige when she saw a dog with a green cloth jacket walk right into the store with its owner. It walked right over the black mat that made the doors open and trotted inside.

Sharron stood up and put on her backpack, and she waved at her mother when she went past the cashiers. She tried to find the dog in the aisles.

She had never seen a dog inside the store. Where was Mrs. Reyes, the owner? Wouldn't she come out and say something?

In the paper aisle, near the napkins and tissues, the woman was holding a box of plastic forks, and the dog was sitting quietly at her feet. His green jacket was belted around his stomach. He wasn't even nosing into her basket of food, which was right next to him.

Sharron pretended to study the paper towels. She stood right next to the dog, but he didn't even look up at her. He was a yellow Lab, his tail still, his ears blond and soft. She reached to pet him, and the woman said, "Sorry, sweetheart, but you shouldn't really distract him, because he's learning. He's going to be a guide dog."

Sharron pulled back her hand, but the woman smiled. "He'd love it if you'd pet him outside, when I'm done. While we're in here, he has to learn to focus all his attention on me, as if I were a blind person shopping, so he can't even look at you."

49

"I'm sorry," Sharron said.

"Don't be sorry," the woman said. She had gray hair in a long braid down her back and wrinkles like a fan at the corners of her eyes. "Just be patient."

Sharron felt her heart beat hard against the bone of her chest. Patient. You'd have to be patient to train a guide dog. "Have patience," Grandma Pat said.

Be patient. Have patience. Patience was something you owned and held inside you. The dog stared straight at the woman's knee and waited.

Sharron waited outside on the bench. She concentrated and listened. Her mother said, "Look at how good Curly's being today. Just perfect. My daughter, Sharron, is outside. She'd probably love to meet you."

The woman said, "I think she has."

"Well, tell her I'll be right out, please, Mrs. Rumer. I finish in ten minutes."

Sharron saw Curly's brown eyes focus on her when he walked up to the bench. Mrs. Rumer said,

"Now's a good time to pet Curly. He deserves some love for being so good in the market."

Sharron reached out her hands and ran them over his ears. They were soft as a baby blanket in her fingers. She said, "Curly. But his fur and tail are so straight."

Mrs. Rumer laughed. "That's why the breeder at the guide-dog school named him Curly. She thought it was funny."

She explained it all to Sharron, and then to Sharron's mother, who sat beside them on the bench when she finished her shift. She got Curly when he was only six weeks old from the guide-dog academy. Each dog was given to someone to raise for a year, to be trained to walk on a leash, to wait, to pay attention to only one person, to never bark or bite, to look out for corners and counters and danger.

"When I'm done training Curly and he's one year old, I'll take him back to the academy and he'll learn much more about being a guide dog, and then he'll graduate and get paired up with a blind person who needs him."

Sharron felt Curly's tail hit her on the knee, again and again, while he wagged it. He was happy that Sharron was petting him, but he was really watching Mrs. Rumer to see what she wanted him to do next.

"Then you'll never see him again?" Sharron said, and she couldn't believe it, but she felt tears in her eyes.

"Oh, I might not," Mrs. Rumer said, but she didn't sound very sad. "If he's given to someone close, I could visit. But really, once I'm done with my job, he truly belongs to his new owner, who will need him for a better life. And I can always remember Curly and the other dogs I've had great years with. I've trained three—Max, Hannah, and now Curly."

"I never saw you before last week," Sharron's mother said now.

"I just moved here from Los Angeles," Mrs. Rumer said. "About a month ago. It was too hard to find space enough for dogs there, but out here in Rio Seco, I found a house with a nice yard."

"A nice yard," Sharron said, putting her cheek next to Curly's damp cold nose. "Curly has a nice yard."

They stood up, and Sharron said, "Will I see you again?"

Her voice was like a torn rag. She heard it herself. Mrs. Rumer put her hand on Sharron's shoulder, her fingers long and strong, and said, "If you're around the store about this time, you'll see us. We'll make it regular."

Mrs. Rumer walked one way with Curly, while Sharron and her mother walked home.

"I'm glad I came to the store today," Sharron said.

Her mother put her arm around Sharron's shoulders. "Did you have a hard day at school?"

Sharron nodded. But she wouldn't tell her mother about Piper and Paige. Instead, she said, "I know what I want to be now. I know exactly how to finish my career project."

Sharron's mother smiled and hugged her closer. "A guide-dog trainer? But, sweetie, that means you always have to say goodbye to a dog you might love."

Sharron said, "Mom, I always had to say goodbye to Daddy, every time he got in the truck and went away. I'm pretty good at that."

She didn't mean to make her mother cry, and her mother didn't let tears run down her face until they got home and she went into her room to take off her uniform. That's when Sharron heard her mother's big long breaths and knew she hadn't said goodbye to Daddy at all. Not yet.

Six

At the school library the next day, Sharron looked for a book about guide-dog training, but the librarian said maybe she'd have to go to the city library downtown to find one.

During the time they worked on their reports, Sharron wrote down a list. Which dogs make the best guide dogs? Golden retrievers and Labrador retrievers. That's funny, she thought, because those dogs loved to swim through waves to get a duck or bird hunted by their masters. That's what it said in her *Dog Breeds of the World* book.

She heard Piper and Paige giggling while they worked. Piper's dog, Carlotta, was a beautiful golden retriever. But she wasn't trained to do anything. Her job is to be pretty and love Piper, Sharron thought. And Paige's rottweiler wouldn't be pretty or a good guide dog at all. Rottweilers were for protection.

At recess, Paige said to Sharron, "Piper says every year you bring your stuffed toy dog to school, and every year you say you're going to get a real dog."

Sharron said, "I *am* going to get a real dog. I'm going to train guide dogs for my career."

Paige said, "I'm going to own a Bath and Body Works store like my mom. Then I can get any kind of lotion I want."

Piper pulled out a bottle of lavender lotion from her pocket. "Paige brought me this because I'm her best friend now. It's called Moonlit Path. I wear it every day. And my mom wears Eternal Serenity."

Paige said, "You can't train guide dogs in an apartment. What'll they do—walk around in circles all day?"

Then Eboni came up behind them and said, "Sharron didn't say she was going to train guide dogs tomorrow. She said for her *career*. And you're not allowed to have lotion or lip gloss at school. The rules say."

Piper put the lotion back in her jacket pocket and said, "Come on, Paige. Let's get out of here."

Sharron got a book about guide dogs on Saturday when her mother took her to the public library. On Sunday she sat on the couch with The Friskative Dog, reading the book and looking at the pictures. It was raining outside. Water ran from the balconies like icicles, and raindrops hit the pool like little rocks.

Some dog breeds had the right temperament or disposition for guide-dog training. Others didn't.

Temperament must mean how you felt about the world. Disposition meant happy or unhappy—she knew that from old Mrs. Reyes at the market, who always said to the checkers and baggers, "Show the world a cheerful disposition."

She would need pictures of the right breeds— Labs and goldens and even boxers—for her report, but she couldn't cut out the photographs from the library books. A magazine! At the market, they had *Dog Fancy* and other magazines. And magazines had ads for dog food. She could cut out pictures from those.

Temperament—humans all had different temperaments, even though they were the same breed, she thought. Juan-Carlos was always talking loud and bragging on the playground, and Ray was always smiling and shooting baskets. Eboni was kind but serious, and she didn't smile but she didn't frown. Mrs. Hernandez was chatty and always hungry, like her parakeet.

I'm—

I'm patient. Quiet. Dreaming?

But I used to be friskative. I used to jump around Daddy's legs when he came home, reaching for the magnet in his jacket pocket. I used to say, "Daddy's home! Let's have handburgers and poptickles for dinner!"

I remember that, Sharron thought, looking at the sheets of rain. I made those words up with him.

We thought burgers were always held in our hands, and Popsicles tickled our tongues.

I remember him sleeping on the couch, and when I asked him why he didn't sleep in the bed sometimes, he said he'd gotten used to dreaming while he sat up in the truck.

Did dogs dream?

Piper and Paige were of a snappish temperament. An unhappy disposition. If they were dogs, they'd be—Chihuahuas? Pekingese?

Her father was a coyote. It came to her suddenly, and she shivered. He was a coyote, loping down the white stripes on the road, looking left and looking right at the houses he passed.

She was surprised when an umbrella appeared outside the big window and her grandmother's face bent to smile into the glass.

Grandma Pat came in smelling of rain and plastic from her raincoat. She left it like an empty shell near the door, a yellow person dripping in the corner.

"It's Sunday!" Sharron's mother said, surprised,

too. "I thought you were heading out to the swap meet for bargains."

Grandma Pat patted The Friskative Dog, her fingernails pink-frosted teardrops on his head and on Sharron's hand. "Your mama and I need to talk, sweetheart," she said. "Go on and give us some privacy for a while."

Sharron stood up and looked out the window at the rain, which blew sideways onto the balcony now and then. Her mother said, "Just hang out in your room with your dog and your book, okay?"

But even with the door closed, Sharron could hear her mother making coffee. She could smell the brown sweet steam when it crept under the door. And she could hear her mother say, "A new driver's license? In Atlanta? How did you find out?"

Grandma Pat said, "I couldn't stand it. I had to hire someone. A detective."

But this wasn't TV. Sharron's ear hurt, she pushed it so hard against her door.

Her mother said, "Another woman?"

Then there were words Sharron couldn't hear. But her grandmother said, "I guess he must have met her on one of those trips when he kept taking recliners to the furniture stores down there."

It was a long time before her mother said anything again. Then she must have dropped something on the floor, with a sharp *crack*. A cup? She said, "Did he think I'd believe he just got lost and never came home?"

"I don't know what he believed," Grandma Pat said. "I don't know what I believe."

"Who is she? She looks about twenty years old."

Sharron smelled the paint on the door, under her cheek, while she listened. How did her mother see the woman? Had Grandma Pat gotten a picture of her?

"This is just a condo," her mother said, crying now. "This is just his name on a lease for a condo. He kept talking about how he didn't want to pay so much taxes, and we'd never be able to afford a house in California." Then her mother must have gone into the bathroom, because Sharron heard that door close.

She heard her grandmother say, "Imagine how I feel. I didn't raise him like that. And he left me, too."

But her grandmother was talking to herself, soft as tissue paper falling on the floor.

When her mother knocked on the door and Sharron came out with The Friskative Dog, her mother's eyes were so red and small they looked like pomegranate seeds. But she said only, "Your grandma Pat wants to take you for a drive. That's why she came over."

Sharron looked at the table, where her grandmother held her white coffee cup like it was a bird. Gently. Her grandmother nodded and said, "I think you need to get some fresh air. You and your dog."

Her grandmother's eyes were not red at all. She smiled and picked up her purse, a big bag that looked like a pretty carpet. It was the only purse she had ever had since Sharron was little, and Sharron said once, "It's like Mary Poppins's bag in the movie!"

Her grandma Pat had laughed and said, "But out here in California, who needs a hat stand and bottles of cough medicine? I've got sunblock and caramel candies and a map, just in case I decide I want to go somewhere like Palm Springs or San Diego."

Sharron's mother was looking out the kitchen window. She isn't going to tell me now, Sharron thought. She's waiting for something.

She tried to picture Atlanta. She looked out the window at the palm trees, sparkling wet. The rain had stopped, and the sun was coming out, and the palm fronds looked like they were covered with dia-monds.

What kind of trees were in Atlanta? Who was this woman? When was her father coming home?

Her grandmother opened the apartment door and said, "Let's get that doggie to a farm where he can run around and chase some sheep."

Sharron looked back at her mother, but her mother's shoulders trembled as if the wind blew out from the sink and pushed at her.

On the stairs behind her grandmother, Sharron said, "Border collies chase sheep, Grandma. This is a yellow Lab. He's a good guide dog."

They got into Grandma Pat's small car, which always smelled of vanilla air freshener from the car wash. Grandma Pat kept her car clean, and the seats were blond and furry like The Friskative Dog.

Sharron looked at the palm trunks whipping past when her grandmother drove toward the freeway. Her father's truck had always smelled of gasoline, sharp like cold wind inside her nose, and of his leather gloves and his favorite wintergreen gum.

How far was it to Atlanta? He always said it took him three days to drive there. But he'd been gone a year.

Grandma Pat didn't talk until they were on the freeway heading past La Reina Market, past Emily Dickinson Elementary School, and toward the orange groves. The hills were purple from the rain, and Sharron remembered her father saying the hills in Rio Seco took on the color of the sky. Golden hot in summer, brown and smoggy in fall, wet and blue-green in winter, and when a storm darkened the sky, the boulders and bushes were the color of bruised clouds.

They passed hundreds of new houses behind a white wall and a sign that said *Citrus Colony*. That's where Paige said she lived—in the Colony, Sharron remembered. And Piper, too. She held The Friska-tive Dog to the window and said, "Bark at Carlotta, okay?"

Then Grandma Pat pointed to the orange groves that stretched away behind the new houses. The groves were in dark green squares, like a quilt sewn by huge hands. "All of Rio Seco used to be orange groves," she said to Sharron, who had heard this story before. "Back in 1920, when my own father came here from New York because he saw a postcard with oranges on the trees and palm trees lining the streets and the sun just as gold as can be. Just like now."

Sharron opened her window to smell the starry white flowers blooming now, even with oranges hanging on the branches still. There was no smell like orange blossoms, her father always said.

She knew her grandmother was taking her to the farm where she'd grown up. She held her soft dog tightly in her arms, and his chest seemed to move with a heartbeat.

Down several miles of narrow rutted road, they stopped at the old white farmhouse. Sharron said, "Oh, no, Grandma! Look at the big house you always wanted to live in someday. So you could sleep upstairs."

The windows were covered with brown squares of wood. The white paint was peeling like alligator scales, and the trees behind the farmhouse were all gray and dead, like ghosts with finger-branches reaching for each other as if to hold on tight.

"I read in the paper where this is all sold for new houses, like the ones on the other side of your school," Grandma Pat said. "So many people are moving here now for big homes."

"Like Paige, this new girl in my class," Sharron

said. "She's always talking about how big her house is. And Piper's always talking about her pool and her bedroom."

Grandma Pat drove slowly down the dirt driveway past the house, toward the groves, and she said, "Well, I know Piper and Paige have never smelled this. Orange blossoms. There's nothing else like it in the world. And your daddy used to love sitting under the trees when he was little. He said when the wind blew and the flowers fell on him, it was snowing white stars."

Sharron started to cry so hard that everything disappeared behind her tears—the trees and the road and even the tiny houses they were stopping in front of now.

Her grandmother put her arms around her and said, "Oh, oh, Sharron, sweetheart. You think he's never coming back. And I can't say for sure that I know that, either. Whatever he has—insomnia, or just plain foolishness—is keeping him away."

Sharron felt her throat burning with the words.

Not insomnia. Not amnesia. How could he have left her, when she could say certain words only to him? "Your gum smells like toothtaste," she used to say when he picked her up, right here, in the orange groves.

Her grandmother waited, and then she smoothed Sharron's hair back on her forehead. "You know, he was a little boy, too. A nine-year-old, like you, riding his bike right here. And when he fell, and he cried, I smelled the ocean on his face, just like on yours now."

Sharron wiped her eyes and looked out the window. Ten tiny houses in a row, where the grove workers had lived. Ten tiny porches where they had sat and sorted through the oranges they'd brought home for themselves, after they'd picked the fruit and packed it into boxes and loaded it onto trucks.

Her father used to talk about how much he loved the flowers but didn't like the oranges, because he'd eaten them all his life.

As if her grandmother knew her thoughts, she

said, "And then, Sharron, he hated the trees and our little house, right after his own father died."

Grandma Pat's husband had died in a truck accident, when he and two other workers were driving big trailers of oranges into the city.

"Then you know I went to night school and learned to type, and I got that job as a secretary, and we moved to the city. And your father went to high school, and then he married your mother and got his own job. He loves to drive. Always has. He drove the trucks through the groves when he was only twelve."

"Twelve!" Sharron looked at the roads between the trees. The Friskative Dog leaned out the window. Then she squinted. She could see something moving farther down the rows, where a clearing of grass led to the hills.

"Well, no one cared how old he was out here," her grandmother said, and then they heard the dog barking.

Sharron and her grandmother got out of the car

and walked down the grove road to the clearing, and Sharron saw the sheep. A hundred or so, milling around like dirty cream clouds brought to earth, and one man with a stick was pushing them toward a pen while his dog ran back and forth, back and forth behind the sheep, as if his nose and barking were his own stick to push them the way he wanted them to go.

"A border collie!" Sharron breathed. The dog was a black-and-white flash, a blur like a small tornado among all those sheep clouds.

She held her own dog to face the spinning, barking collie.

The man smiled at Grandma Pat and said, "You come to see your trees again, eh?"

She smiled back and said to him, "I wanted to show my granddaughter how big a yard can be."

Sharron frowned, but her grandmother said, "That's Enrique, the sheepherder. He's from Peru. He lives here, with the sheep, and moves his house with them when they need to go to a new place."

He had a small trailer, and when the sheep were inside the corral, Enrique sat on a stone and lit a pipe. His dog studied Sharron and her grandmother for a moment and seemed to cock his head at The Friskative Dog, but then lay with his head down on the grass beside Enrique's boots. A border collie lived to herd animals—that's what the dog-breeds book said. If there were no sheep to herd, he would herd children, nipping at their heels and barking to make sure they stayed together. Sharron smiled at the tired dog; his eyes had closed immediately once the sheep were inside their corral.

Grandma Pat waved goodbye, and when they were driving back down the grove road, the sky darkening again as if it might rain, she said, "When I got that job, and when your father married your mother, I bought my own trailer. Bigger than that one, but it's still a trailer."

Her grandmother lived in a mobile-home park, because she'd always said houses were too expensive, and she was alone, anyway. Sharron glanced back at

Enrique's tiny trailer, with rust streaks at the screen door. She said, "He must not stay inside much."

Grandma Pat said, "When I first lived here, there was Pablo. He was the sheepherder then, from Spain. He stayed in the fields for fifteen years, and my father said those men liked to walk all day, and they liked to be alone, and they sent all their money back to their families in Spain. Now Enrique must do the same, because he's been here a long time. I come back sometimes to see my trees. My little old house."

The small grove houses looked like tiny churches in the distance behind the car, with their steep roofs and boarded-up doors.

"But today I wanted to come because I wanted you to see that dog. Every sheepherder that works those fields has always had a great dog. And you'll have one, someday."

"Someday," Sharron said. The Friskative Dog rode on her lap, sitting high to see over the dashboard.

"Someday your father may come back," her grand-mother said, her voice very quiet now. "But someday your mother might not still be waiting for him. Do you understand?"

"I don't know." Sharron felt her eyes blur again, and she wiped hard at her eyelids. They felt like paper under her fingers.

"Sweetheart, what I'm saying is that your father is my son, but now your mother is my daughter, and I would like us to stay a family. I want you both for my family. Now and always. It doesn't matter whether your father comes back—I will never go anywhere far from you. I will always be here."

"I'm going to wait for him," Sharron whispered. "But I'm going to think about a dog. Someday."

Seven

● ● ● ● ● ● ●

But in the morning, when it was time for school, someday seemed too far away. Sharron and her mother ate eggs and toast, and then her mother got on her uniform and said, "I'll walk you to school."

While her mother was in the bathroom, Sharron looked at the guide-dog book and put it in her backpack so she could work on her report during lunchtime. Then she looked at The Friskative Dog. He was a yellow Lab. He could wear a green jacket. She wrapped a green dish towel around him, tied it on with a piece of yarn, and moved him along the floor with his purple leash. When she heard her mother turn off the blow-dryer, Sharron put the dog into her backpack, too, and even though she knew he might have trouble breathing if she closed it, she zipped the top shut nearly all the way.

She knew she wasn't supposed to take him to school. There was no show-and-tell or pet parade or Day as a Star in fourth grade. But her dog was part of her career project. He was a yellow Lab puppy. Yellow Labs make good guide dogs.

And after school, she would walk to the market and show The Friskative Dog to Mrs. Rumer and Curly, and she would ask Mrs. Rumer exactly what kind of training would be good for a puppy.

The Friskative Dog rode on her back. She could feel him while she walked beside her mother on the way to school. But he didn't feel the way he had when she brought him to school in first grade, or even last year. Her dog felt lighter now, smaller.

I'm bigger. Even my backpack is bigger, she realized.

He's a puppy. He would be a puppy forever, Sharron thought, running her hand along the chain-link fence to collect the dew and feeling the slap of oleander leaves against her knees when they came to a narrow part of the sidewalk.

"Keep your jacket zipped up today," her mother said, looking off at the clouds over the hills, just above where the orange trees would be.

"Did you ever go see where Daddy and Grandma used to live?" Sharron asked.

Her mother glanced down, her eyes gray as the sidewalk, as the sky, as the blank space of an Etch A Sketch, and Sharron was suddenly nervous. "A few times," her mother said finally, when they were across the street from school. "We sat on his little tiny porch and he gave some snacks to that sheepdog that lived out there."

Sharron froze in surprise. The border collie? She didn't want to correct her mother. She said, "Daddy had a dog out there, I bet, when he was a kid, huh?"

Her mother said, "He had one that used to run through the groves with him and play. But there were coyotes out there, and the dog ran away. He either got killed by coyotes or he decided he wanted to live with them. Grandma Pat didn't let your father get another dog, because he was so sad." Her mother reached down and tightened the rubber band on Sharron's braid. "That's why those sheep have to stay inside the corral and be guarded by the sheepdog. Because of the coyotes. Your dad always wanted a puppy, and he never got to have one."

Then her mother kissed her on the forehead—it felt like a small damp flower brushing along her skin—and walked to La Reina Market.

Sharron waited for the crossing guard, and when she stood in front of the playground fence, she reached back and put her fingers inside the opening of her backpack. She could feel an ear of The Friska-tive Dog.

No one could hurt him. No coyote. No hawk. He couldn't run away.

He would be perfect to train, until—maybe until her mother gave her The Big Surprise, which might be . . . well, what if the surprise *was* a dog?

Her mother waved goodbye again at the corner,

and Sharron made sure the zipper of her backpack was nearly closed. But she could feel her dog's nose poking out for air. His black leathery nose was cold and damp from the morning. Just like a real dog.

He stayed quietly in her backpack all morning, under her desk. She could see his nose and even a part of his eye shining up at her when she reached into her desk for pencils or an eraser or paper.

He was being so good. Patient. He was waiting for her to tell him what to do.

She whispered to him, "You can come out at lunch. You can stretch your legs. You've been quiet all morning."

She listened to Mrs. Monson do the math problems on the board. To train a dog meant you'd teach him. Like a teacher, but for a dog. A dog you could sleep with, be friends with, and love.

Then you'd have to let him go, to take care of someone else.

Sharron thought, I don't know if I could let my

dog go. Even to help a blind person. I don't know if I could say goodbye and never see him again.

The bell rang for lunch, and she picked up her whole backpack, not just her lunch bag, to go outside.

At the picnic tables, she sat with Eboni and Brittany. Juan-Carlos and Ray ate their lunches so quickly the Cheeto dust was still orange on their fingertips when they threw away their sacks and started playing basketball. Piper and Paige ate at another table. Sharron could hear their voices like mockingbirds sitting on a telephone wire, talking back and forth.

When she was finished with her peanut butter and jelly sandwich, she opened the backpack and took out The Friskative Dog, but she held him on her lap. "Shhhh," she said to Eboni and Brittany, and felt her finger at her own lips. "He's training to be a guide dog. He can't get distracted. He has to sit here on my lap and not move, even if there are lots of kids around."

"Are you allowed to have a toy here?" Brittany said.

"He's not a toy!" Sharron said.

"But we can't even have lip gloss or lotion or Game Boys," Eboni said. "You have to make sure the yard-duty teacher doesn't see him."

No one saw him on her lap, because everyone was watching Juan-Carlos and Ray play basketball on the court. They were shouting and spinning in the air.

The Friskative Dog was so good. He didn't move.

She ran her hand along his green jacket. She touched his collar, and Eboni said, "I remember your dog from when we were in first grade. He's always had the same collar, huh?"

Brittany said, "But he doesn't have his name on his collar."

Sharron saw Piper and Paige throw away their empty juice boxes, and when they turned back toward the picnic tables, she slid her dog back inside the backpack and whispered, "Good boy. You did a great job."

After school, she walked quickly to La Reina Market. How could she have forgotten to get him an identification tag! All dogs had to have ID tags.

She waited on the corner, and a big truck went past, lifting her hair with its wind. Sharron thought about her father's new driver's license. What kind of tags did humans have, besides cards in their wallets? And rings on their fingers?

On the bench in front of the store, Mrs. Rumer was sitting with Curly! Sharron ran over to the bench, but then she remembered, and she stopped and waited until Mrs. Rumer said, "Okay, Sharron, you can come and pet Curly. Curly, you can say hello to Sharron."

Curly took his eyes from Mrs. Rumer and licked Sharron's face, licked her hands, and even licked at the top of her backpack when she sat down.

Sharron pulled out The Friskative Dog, and

Curly studied the brown eyes and the black leather nose and the ears that looked just like his own. He cocked his head sideways, and his nostrils moved quickly.

Then he licked The Friskative Dog, too. Curly sat back down and eyed Mrs. Rumer, who smiled and said, "What a good, friendly boy, Curly."

Sharron said, "You're a great guide-dog trainer."

Mrs. Rumer laughed, and the two fans of her wrinkles showed at the corners of her eyes. Her eyes were as blue as glass cleaner. She said, "Sharron, what really happens is that dogs train people."

"What do you mean?" Sharron let The Friskative Dog down off her lap, on his leash, and he sat staring out at the parking lot, just like Curly.

"When dogs are puppies, they squirm around with their littermates. Their brothers and sisters. Then their mother teaches them who's boss. She is. But soon the little puppies realize they're a pack."

"A pack sounds scary."

"No, no, a pack just means they're a group of

dogs. And one has to be the leader, the boss, because that's how dogs are. And people."

Sharron watched Curly and The Friskative Dog. She heard her mother's voice inside and Mrs. Reyes, the store owner, talking to the driver of a truck delivering tortillas.

"A store has an owner. A class has a teacher. A family has—" Sharron stopped, thinking of her father and mother, and then she pulled her dog onto her lap.

"A family has two leaders, or sometimes one, or sometimes it's a grandmother, or even an uncle or aunt. But every family has a leader, too. Just like a pack." Mrs. Rumer ran her fingers over Curly's head and rubbed his shoulder, and his skin jumped near his leg. Like a shiver, but a shiver that meant he liked something.

"So Curly left his pack," Sharron said. "All the guide dogs leave their pack." She didn't want to talk about her father, or her mother. She wanted to talk about dogs.

Mrs. Rumer nodded. "Curly came to me, and he tested me. I had to learn with the very first dog I trained to be firm, and not to change my mind, and to let him know who the leader of this pack was." She stood up. "We're a pack of two. Really, that's enough sometimes." Curly was paying attention to her now, not to the tortilla truck or the pigeon on the roof or The Friskative Dog, whom he'd been eyeing now and then. "I see your doggie is well behaved, too. You're doing a good job."

Sharron stood up, too. "Thank you," she said. She petted Curly one more time, and then she went inside the store.

Her mother smiled and said, "I see you went home already and got your doggie. Did he decide he needed some dog biscuits?"

Sharron didn't want to tell her mother she'd taken The Friskative Dog to school. She said, "Mom, can I have my month allowance early? I want to get him an ID tag."

Mrs. Reyes said, "What for? Doesn't he know his name?" She was signing a piece of paper about the tortillas.

Sharon touched his ear and said to Mrs. Reyes, "Just in case."

She took the five dollars her mother gave her and walked next door to the little shop where Mr. Abdul made keys and repaired shoes. She pointed to the tag on the board, the one shaped like a bone, and wrote TFD. She remembered when she couldn't spell his name, back when she was in first grade. But then she crossed out the initials and wrote *Friskative*. Then she wrote her phone number, so his tag would be just like Curly's.

Mr. Abdul brought the tag to her after a short time. He said, "What is this—Frisk-a-tive?"

"That's his name," Sharron said, and she put the silver tag on her dog's collar and waited on the bench for her mother.

* * *

That night, while her mother was in her room on the phone with Leila, Sharron left her dog sleeping on her bed, and she went into the dark kitchen. She found her mother's purse, took out her wallet, and looked at her cards. Driver's license—the picture was old. Her mother's hair was longer and her eyes darker in the picture. She was smiling. Karen Joy Baker.

She saw one silver credit card with her mother's name, and a library card, and a card with things about La Reina Market, and a card for the PTA for Emily Dickinson Elementary.

That was it.

Sharron put the wallet back in her mother's purse. She opened a few drawers in the kitchen, and the second one down from the silverware drawer had her report cards, a long typed letter that said *Palm Gardens* on the top and was about their apartment, and then she found her papers.

Everyone had papers.

Her birth certificate. Her weight and height

86

and the time she was born. She was twenty inches long. And a paper that said *License of Marriage*. But it wasn't a card. It said their names, and where they were born, and the date of their marriage. There were other names. Patricia Baker. Leila Ramos. Under their names it said *Witnesses*.

She had heard Leila say today at the store, "Are you going to file papers?"

What did that mean?

She slid the papers back into the drawer and went to her bedroom. She lay under her covers, with her dog warm beside her, and thought. Cats and dogs had papers. Rabbits and chickens didn't. Butterflies and ladybugs. Only dogs stayed in a pack. You never saw a pack of cats, or a pack of rabbits. She and her mother were a pack now. A family. And The Friska-tive Dog.

Wild animals had packs sometimes. Deer and skunks and possums? The possum who drank from the pool had seven babies.

Coyotes were supposed to run in packs, but she'd

only seen the one, loping down that hot street, along the painted line.

Her father was in another state. He had a new driver's license. A new wife? No. No new family. No new name.

When a dog was lost, if it had no collar and you found it, you would give it a different name. How could you call every name until the dog seemed to recognize his own? Shep Blackie Fluffy Scout Teddy Maggie Chloe Bear Spot Speedy Spindlemutt?

What had her father said to the woman he met?

My name is—

I'm—

You can call me—

Sharron put her head under her pillow. Only one person in the world can call him Daddy, she thought, and that's me. No one else.

Eight

● ● ● ● ● ● ●

In the morning, it was foggy. She thought about the border collie moving the sheep through the fields, where the fog would cover the grass.

The fog hung over the pool, making diamonds on the black iron railings, swirling around the carports. The empty carports looked like horse stables. The border collie would run away from here, from apartments, because he wouldn't have anyone to herd, any room to run.

Like her father.

A magazine was on the kitchen table, she saw, and her mother came out of the bathroom with her uniform on and new earrings in her ears. Silver hoops with tiny dangling hearts. "I got us each something yesterday," her mother said, smiling. "Since your dog got a new tag. I got you this to help with your project, and I got myself earrings to help me feel better."

She hugged Sharron hard and said, "You can cut out pictures after school." The magazine was called *BARK*. On the cover was a dalmatian with a Santa hat. Every page inside had pictures of dogs: golden retrievers, boxers, pugs, greyhounds and dalmatians and Labrador retrievers, yellow and black.

"Thanks, Mom," Sharron said. She saw the price on the magazine. $4.95. Between that and her early allowance, her mother had already spent ten dollars on her this week. "I love it. I'll put it in my room."

But in her bedroom, she put *BARK* and The Friskative Dog inside her backpack, next to her homework.

He waited just as the day before, under her desk, and everything was fine until lunch. She took her backpack to the picnic tables, but Piper and Paige were already sitting next to Eboni and Brittany, and when Sharron sat down, Piper said, "You must have a big lunch in there."

Sharron opened her backpack on her lap, sliding out just her lunch bag so they wouldn't see her dog. Piper has to be leader of the pack, she thought. Every day. She can't just let us sit here and laugh. She has to show off for Paige now, too.

She pulled out her magazine and said to Eboni and Brittany, "My mom got me this. For my project on training dogs."

They turned the pages of *BARK*, while Paige and Piper whispered and ate their Lunchables and waited for Sharron to notice that they weren't looking. She noticed.

She said, "Look at this! A leash with an umbrella! That's so cute if you were walking your dog in the rain."

"What's this?" Eboni said, pointing to an advertisement with a small dog standing next to a long wooden box planted with grass. He was a beagle who looked as if he were smiling.

"Hey!" Brittany laughed. "Look!" She read the words. *"Real grass balcony bathroom for apartment dogs."*

Sharron laughed, too. "That's for people who live in a big city in a tall building and they don't want to go down the elevator to take their dogs outside!"

Piper was listening now, because she said loudly, "Like your dog? Your apartment dog that isn't even real?"

Sharron pulled open the zipper and brought out The Friskative Dog onto her lap. She said, "He's real enough to help me learn how to be a guide-dog trainer. Dogs train us to train them."

"Oh, my God," Piper said, laughing and pointing at the dog. "That is so pathetic. Look, Paige, he has a dish towel on his back."

Sharron looked down at her dog, his tag glinting in the sun, and for the first time she saw how he looked to the others. His ears were frazzled and fuzzy from his baths. His fur was worn down around his neck from all the nights she had held him so tightly, and a bald patch showed under his chin from where his collar rubbed. The dish towel looked dumb, with the yarn wrapped around his belly.

But in the light, she could see clear inside his eyes, into the shiny gold bars like sun rays around the brown. Something shifted inside there. Something moved.

Sharron said, "You know what, Piper? This isn't your pack."

Piper folded her arms and stuck out her chin like she always did. "What are you talking about, with your loser stuffed dog?"

Sharron said, "He's teaching me how to train dogs. In the whole class, I'm the only one who's already practicing my career project." She looked at the court. "Except Ray, since he's playing basketball." She looked at Eboni and Brittany.

Brittany said, "I'm going to be a hairdresser in a big salon. But I can't cut hair yet."

Eboni said, "I'm going to be a nurse like my mom. But I've only practiced on my dolls."

Sharron saw Piper opening her mouth again and

she thought, I'd better be the leader. I'd better talk first. She said, "Well, Piper, you're supposed to be staying home and raising kids, right? But you're here at school. And Paige doesn't own a Bath and Body Works yet. So my dog can look however he wants to—he's helping me with my career."

Paige said, "So that's the dog you're always talking about? That's sad." She looked at Piper. "My dog can do tricks like jump in the air and roll over."

Sharron said, "Those tricks are cool to watch, but they don't help anyone. My dog is training me. He's training me to be patient, and I'm training him to help someone else."

Paige said, "Well, he can't roll over." But her voice was uncertain.

But Piper was furious. She put her hands on her hips, and her fingers curled up like claws. Not paws. "How can you train something with stuffing in his head? And buttons for eyes?"

Sharron hugged him close, bending over so the

yard-duty teacher wouldn't see, and put him inside his home for the day. She zipped the zipper most of the way, because he needed to breathe, and she couldn't see her dog's nose—only his furry forehead.

Just then the bell began to beep and beep and beep. A fire drill! They all scrambled around to find their classes and line up, and Sharron realized she was still carrying the magazine. When they filed into the classroom after the fire drill was over, Mrs. Monson said, "Sharron, we don't read magazines during schooltime. Put it in your desk."

Piper rolled her eyes at Sharron.

During the last period, they had kickball for PE, and Mrs. Monson sent Piper and Paige back to the classroom to get the ball and bring it to the playground. They held hands while they walked, and when they came back with the ball, they were whispering and giggling. Sharron told herself, They're a pack of two. That's okay, as long as they don't have to bother me every minute.

After kickball was over, it was nearly time for

school to end. Mrs. Monson rushed around giving out the homework and the spelling list, and Sharron didn't even put the papers in her backpack, because she didn't want to open the zipper until she got to the market. She didn't want Piper and Paige to see The Friskative Dog again, to make fun of his eyes and closed mouth and leathery nose.

She hoped he could breathe.

She heard Piper's mother picking up Piper and Paige, heard them laughing, and she heard Eboni's mother call to her from the parking lot. She walked the other way, toward the crossing guard, and then down the street to La Reina Market.

When she got to the parking lot, Mrs. Rumer was sitting on the bench with Curly at her feet, and she held up a tiny green jacket. Sharron began to run. A green jacket for The Friskative Dog! Mrs. Rumer was definitely in the family pack! She was smiling and waving, and Curly was wagging his tail.

Sharron sat down on the bench, opened her backpack, and her dog was gone.

***

At first, it felt like crickets were scurrying up and down her backbone. She looked inside again. Folder, eraser, pencils, and notebook. *BARK* magazine. She reached inside and felt around with her hand, and then, inside her stomach, it felt like someone was tearing pieces of wet paper.

"He's gone," she said to Mrs. Rumer. "He's gone."

On the zipper was a tuft of yellow yarn. That's what she'd tied his green jacket with. The fake jacket. The dish towel. So pathetic. They called her dog pathetic.

He had to have fallen out of her backpack during the fire drill.

Sharron put her face in her hands and cried, and the tears were hot on her fingers. She felt the salt sting where she had a cut from kickball.

The fire drill. They all lined up near the back fence, where no one ever went.

Suddenly her mother was there, bending over her, and Mrs. Rumer was saying, "She lost her dog.

Curly and I had brought him a gift, but I didn't think she'd have her dog with her."

Her mother lifted up her face and said, "Sharron, how did you get home so fast to get The Friskative Dog? It's only been ten minutes since school got out."

Sharron cried even harder. She didn't want to tell her mother she'd taken him to school. Her mother said, "I don't know what to do. I can't leave, because Leila's not back from lunch and there's no one else here."

Mrs. Rumer said, "Sharron, Sharron, honey, do you want me to take you back to the school to look?"

"Back to school?" Sharron's mother said. "You took him to school?"

Sharron said miserably, "I took him to school because I was training him, and he was training me. Now he's gone forever. I think he fell out of my backpack during the fire drill today." She cried again.

"Oh, Sharron, what were you thinking?" her mother said.

Curly's nose was cold and wet in her fingers. Curly licked the salty tears from Sharron's hand.

Mrs. Rumer said gently, "It's hard to train anyone if they stay inside all the time. Sometimes you have to let someone outside and take a chance. How about if Curly and I take Sharron back to the playground and look for The Friskative Dog? Curly knows what he looks like. They're acquainted now."

"Oh, please, Mom? We have to hurry before the sprinklers come on after school. He might get soaked."

Her mother nodded, her own eyes so shiny with tears they looked to Sharron like two small mirrors in the sun. "I can't seem to do anything right," her mother said, and Mrs. Rumer put her hand on Sharron's mother's arm.

"Well, now, you're working and coming home, and Sharron took her own dog to school, so I don't see that you did anything wrong," she said. "We'll find that mischievous little guy."

They walked quickly along the sidewalk, Curly alert and watching every bush and tree and car and person. Sharron's backpack felt like an empty snail shell. She looked ahead and saw that the crossing guard was just getting into her own car, and only a few people were left near the fence.

She ran toward the far side of the playground, where the classes had all lined up for the fire drill, but even near the ivy and trees at the very back of the school, she saw nothing but shiny fruit-snack wrappers and a shard of paper cup, white as bone. When she looked up, Curly was running toward her. Mrs. Rumer had let him off the leash, and Curly leapt and galloped over the dry yellow grass toward Sharron as if they were playing fetch.

She nearly fell on the sand near the swing set, she wanted to cry so badly. She would never have a live dog like Curly to race around her legs, to rub his head along her hand as if to say, "Come on, let's run!" And now she had lost her real dog, her best friend, and her eyes kept scanning back and forth along the grass, the fence, the picnic tables that looked so sad and scarred when no one was sitting there eating lunch.

Lunch. The girls had seen her dog at lunch. Eboni and Brittany, Piper and Paige. What if one of them had told Mrs. Monson, and Mrs. Monson had taken The Friskative Dog from Sharron's backpack because she wasn't allowed to have him? But her backpack had been under her desk all afternoon, after lunch. And Mrs. Monson wouldn't have done that without telling her.

Mrs. Rumer called Curly, who ran back to her. Sharron walked slowly back toward the gate, since she saw the custodian coming that way with the keys. Eboni and Brittany were her friends—they wouldn't have told anyone about her dog. They were in her school pack. Piper or Paige might have told someone, but who? The Friskative Dog had to have fallen out of her backpack during the fire drill.

The custodian frowned at her and said, "Did you lose something? So far today, I found two sweaters, three lunch bags, and a jacket that says *All-Star*."

"Did you find a dog?" Sharron asked.

He raised his eyebrows. "A dog? Nope. I would have noticed a dog. Little, like to fit on a pencil eraser?"

Sharron held out her hands and started crying again. "No. The size of a real yellow Lab puppy, about six weeks old."

"Well, here comes your dog now!" the custodian said, smiling, and then Curly raced over to Sharron again and nudged her knee.

On the sidewalk, Mrs. Rumer told Curly, "Settle down now, and get back on your leash. That was an unusual circumstance. You had to be a rescue dog. You had to rescue Sharron with some love."

She hooked the leash onto Curly's collar and took Sharron's hand, and they walked along the chain-link fence where the leaves were piled like brown feathers.

Near the market, Sharron's mother waited at the red light across the street from them, and she looked anxiously at Sharron. "Did you find him?!" she called across the moving cars, and Sharron shook her head.

She didn't want to say the words.

He's gone.

If he fell out of her backpack, another kid could have picked him up from the playground and taken him home, and she would probably never see The Friskative Dog again. He would sleep on someone else's bed, in someone's else's arms.

He was gone.

The light changed and her mother met them in the middle of the crosswalk and hugged Sharron tight. She thanked Mrs. Rumer then turned Sharron around with her arms and they walked to the other side, to start for home.

Nine

●●●●●●●●●

Sharron couldn't sleep all night. Her mother had made linguini with butter and Parmesan cheese, her favorite, the cheese like snow. Her mother had called Grandma Pat, and Grandma Pat had said on the phone, "I'll come over tomorrow afternoon and we'll get you a new dog. We'll get you a better dog, okay?"

When someone's dog died, sometimes they talked about how a new puppy or dog would make them feel better. But sometimes people never got another dog, because a new dog would never be the same.

"Why didn't you ever let Daddy get a new dog

after his dog ran away?" she said into the phone, and she heard her own voice mean and low.

Her mother frowned and said, "Sharron. Don't talk to your grandmother that way."

Grandma Pat was quiet for long enough that Sharron heard someone across the courtyard slam a door. Then Grandma Pat said, "I didn't want him to lose another one. He took things so hard. Just like you."

"Well, now he's gone, and my dog is gone. I don't know how to take things easy."

Sharron handed the phone back to her mother without speaking, and went into her room and closed the door.

She heard her mother's voice through the wall. She heard her mother's voice change when she talked to Leila. She heard her mother call someone else. Then everything in the apartment was quiet.

Sharron rolled around on her bed and cried silently, so no one would hear in all the walls and doors of the Palm Gardens apartment building. All the people inside the rooms, like honeycombs full of bees. A pack of bees. A pack of apartments. Doors and railings and walkways. Mrs. Hernandez's parakeet chirping behind the glass.

Mrs. Rumer had said today you can't train anyone or anything by keeping it inside all the time. But Sharron should never have taken The Friskative Dog to school. She ran her hands over the sheets again and again where he usually lay next to her, and they were wet and cold and wrinkled from her anger and tears and her hands bunching up the emptiness.

She tried to think of math. Estimating. How many people were in Palm Gardens? Two or three people in each apartment—but then she thought of how there were three people in this apartment before her father left, and she cried even harder. Where did the tears come from? Inside her brain?

She crept outside to the front window and looked at the cold moon above the courtyard. One day, when she was very small, she'd tried to balance a water glass on the balcony, and it had fallen to the cement. She'd thought her father would be angry, but he showed her how the glass sparkled, and then he swept it into a dustpan, saying, "You broke that to slivereens, didn't you?"

They're both gone. My heart is broken into slivereens, Sharron thought, putting her face to the dark window.

In the morning, her mother opened the door and said, "Why aren't you up yet, sweetheart? I heard your alarm clock go off. I have a special breakfast for you, since yesterday was such a bad day."

Sharron could smell pancakes. Her father always smelled like pancakes. Her mother didn't make them often now that he was gone, because even the syrup made her sad, Sharron knew. She'd heard her mother say that to Grandma Pat once.

Her mother's long hair leaned into the doorway with her. The silver earrings swayed and winked in the sunlight. Her mother's fingernails were painted pink like candy hearts. Her mother was feeling better, Sharron thought.

But I'm not.

"I'm not going to school. I feel sick. I feel like I'm going to throw up."

Her mother sat on the bed and tried to smooth the wrinkles of the sheet next to Sharron. The sheet looked tangled as a bird's nest. "Sharron. You can't give up now. I didn't give up."

"Give up on what?" Sharron wanted to know how her mother felt about her father. No one had told her anything about Atlanta.

Her mother said, "I didn't give up on our life. I don't know if your father's coming back or not, but I didn't stay in bed and quit my job and cry all day, because I have you. I love you. Even if everyone seems to be disappearing, we have to get through the day, with each other."

Sharron stared at the wall. The light-green paint. Her mother's voice through the wall. As long as her mother had someone to talk to, she could get up in the morning, even when Sharron had heard her crying much of the night.

But I don't have anyone to talk to now. I can't use my special words with Daddy. How could he leave like that, just decide he didn't want to be here anymore? How could he stay in Atlanta, when he always said he hated going so far on that run? He used to say, "I have to make a run to Atlanta," and I used to say, "But your feet just push the pedals up and down. Your feet never go anywhere." And one time he said, "Well, they sure get tired anyway."

How could he get tired of her? His girl?

She set her mouth and said, "I'm not going today. I'll go tomorrow."

She didn't want to see any of them. Her friends, her enemies, the kids she didn't even know who might have taken her dog. No one.

"I can't stay home just like that," her mother said.

"I'm almost ten now, Mom," Sharron said. "I can stay here by myself with the door locked."

"Almost ten isn't grown." Her mother frowned and pushed the hair off Sharron's forehead. "I'll call Grandma Pat and ask her to come by before lunch to stay with you. That's only about two hours. She told me she had some important business this morning."

Sharron nodded and turned away into her pillow.

She heard her mother open and close the refrigerator, heard plates go back into the cabinet. "We'll have to eat these pancakes later," her mother called. "When you feel better. I put the batter away, and I'll bring home some sausage to go with them. And apples."

The door closed. The lock clicked.

She could hear the voices from the courtyard. She could even hear her mother's footsteps on the pebbled stairs. Hollow sound of shoes.

She didn't want to look out the window and see her mother's hair moving down the street toward the store, so she put her head under the pillow for a long time.

When she woke up, the phone was ringing. She

ran blindly toward the kitchen. Her mother must be calling to check on her. The clock said ten-thirteen.

"Hello?" she breathed.

"Hello," a woman said. "I'm calling about a dog. This phone number was on his tag. His name must be Friskative."

"You found him?!!" Sharron said.

"Yes," the woman said. "I found him this morning. It looked like someone must have cared about him or they wouldn't have put a tag on his collar. He was outside my house. Would you like to come and get him?"

Sharron looked at the empty kitchen, the sun shining on the clean sink. "Where was he?" she said.

The woman paused. "Well, he wasn't in a very nice place," she said finally. "I'm sure he would be happy to be home with you, if he's your dog."

"He's my dog," Sharron said.

Then she took a deep breath. She couldn't ask the woman to come here and bring the dog, because the woman was a stranger. "I'll come as soon as I can."

The woman gave her the address: 1467 Orange Tree Circle.

"I'll be home until about two today," she said. "Or you could come get him next week, when I get back from vacation."

"I'll be there today," Sharron said, and she hung up the phone.

She called Grandma Pat, but the answering machine came on. She couldn't call the store and ask her mother, because this address sounded far away, and her mother wouldn't be able to borrow a car. She called her grandmother again, close to crying, but again the machine answered the phone.

Sharron got dressed and put on her backpack. She went outside to sit on the pebbled stairs. She wished she knew where Mrs. Rumer lived. Mrs. Rumer had a car. Mrs. Rumer would do anything for a dog.

The neighbors' doors were all closed, except Mrs. Hernandez's, and she didn't drive or speak English. Her parakeet talked to itself in the window.

Grandma Pat was supposed to be here by lunch,

but what if she came late and the woman was gone? Then Sharron might not get The Friskative Dog back for a long time.

Mrs. Monson had a car. She could walk to school, like she always did, and show this address to Mrs. Monson. Mrs. Monson might be disappointed when she found out how he'd gotten lost because Sharron had brought the dog to school, but maybe at lunchtime Mrs. Monson would take her to this house. Before two.

She walked slowly toward school. Everything felt different at this time of morning, and even the cars passing her on the street sounded faster. Her mother would be angry because she left the house. Everyone was going to be angry, and all because she'd brought her dog to school to train. She pictured the dogs in *BARK* magazine while she walked, and Curly running toward her yesterday on the playground. She even pictured a dog lifting his leg over the silly balcony lawn planter in the magazine.

But when she got to school, it was morning

recess, and all the kids swarmed the playground, laughing and shouting and hitting the tetherball and running between the trees like horses.

As she got close to the fence, she saw people staring at her. No one came to school this late. She saw Eboni and Brittany, Piper and Paige, Ray and Juan-Carlos, and all the others in her class, and all the bigger kids she didn't know, and the little kids she didn't know, and she wondered who had taken her dog from the playground. She froze by the fence and turned her back to the chain link. She heard her name. She heard the bell ring three times for the end of recess. She heard the voices disappear as everyone went back inside the classrooms.

Eboni's mother said, "Sharron? Girl, what are you doing on the wrong side of the fence looking so sad?"

Eboni's mother had parked her car at the back gate. She was carrying a bag from Del Taco. She said, "I couldn't make Eboni's lunch today, so I went just now and got her favorite burritos. Sharron! Why are you crying?"

114

Sharron buried her face into Eboni's mother's white uniform. Eboni's mother smelled like vitamins and vanilla perfume.

She told Eboni's mother about yesterday and the fire drill, and Eboni's mother said, "Your dog got lost? Eboni has been telling me for years about your dog and his cute little ears and tail."

Sharron nodded. She said, "Someone found my dog today. They called my house. But I can't go get him. My mother doesn't have a car."

Eboni's mother looked at her watch. "You know what? I'm on my lunch break early, because I wanted to get these burritos here. Let me go and bring this bag to Eboni, and then we might have time. Is this the address?"

She studied the piece of paper Sharron gave her. "This is right around the corner, in those new Citrus Colony houses. You wait right here by the fence until I come back."

Eboni's mother's car was a red Mustang with black leather seats. Sharron felt the leather warm under her palms. Eboni's mother played the radio loud and said, "We'll just scoot right up this road and then on to the other side of the hill. My brothers and I used to go to those orange groves all the time when we were little. We used to play war with the old oranges." She smiled and winked at Sharron. "Once those oranges fall on the ground and dry out, girl, they make good weapons."

They turned into a set of gates that read *Citrus Colony*, with two orange trees on either side. "Last oranges left around here," Eboni's mother said, looking again at the address. She drove slowly down the first street. The houses were all two stories, beige or brown, with big garages in the front and stripes of green lawn on either side. There were basketball hoops and soccer nets in some driveways. There were big trash cans out by each curb.

"Here it is," Eboni's mother said, and she stopped in front of a beige house with pumpkins and Indian corn on the porch, and even a bale of hay.

Sharron's heart pounded harder than her knuckles knocking on the door. Eboni's mother said, "Wow, look at that fountain. It sounds like a waterfall."

A woman opened the door holding The Friskative Dog! She smiled and said, "Well, that didn't take long!"

Eboni's mother put out her hand and said, "I'm Desirae. This is Sharron. She's my daughter's friend."

The woman said, "I'm Nancy Cates. I found this little guy in my trash can this morning when I went out to the curb. I'd put the trash out last night, but I was dropping in this morning's milk carton and just happened to see his ear sticking out. Pretty lucky."

Sharron held her dog close to her face and wouldn't let tears come. She didn't have any left, she thought. His ears were soft on her cheek, and his tag was cold.

"Pretty lucky you didn't have banana peels and yucky stuff in there," Eboni's mother said.

Sharron buried her nose in his fur and smelled

something sweet and purple. Something she'd smelled before. She froze. She breathed in deeply and closed her eyes.

Moonlit Path.

The lotion Paige had given Piper from her mother's store.

"Are you okay, Sharron?" Nancy Cates said.

Sharron said, "I don't know. Do any girls live on this block?"

Nancy Cates looked like a grandmother. She said, "Well, there's a little girl about your age in that house two doors down. She has a big reddish dog who's always pooping on people's lawns, and her mother makes her carry a plastic bag now when she walks her, because some of the neighbors complained." Nancy Cates smiled. "The dog has a funny name, I think. I've heard her yelling at it. Something like Carolina."

Ten

●●●●●●●●

Eboni's mother drove slowly down the hill toward Sharron's neighborhood. Sharron held her dog tightly, even though the smell of the lotion was strong. Her dog's ears were matted. "I'll wash you when we get home," she whispered to him.

"Look at all the palm trees sparkly clean from the rain," Eboni's mother said. They could see Emily Dickinson Elementary School, La Reina Market with the crown sign above it, and the row of apartment buildings on Palm Avenue. Sharron could see the small houses on their narrow streets all along the other side of Palm Avenue. If she had time, she could count them like the stones in the apartment steps. Their backyards were like green dish towels laid out behind the fences.

The Friskative Dog's dish-towel jacket was gone. Piper must have thrown it away.

Eboni's mother said, "So you know who took him, right?"

Sharron nodded.

Eboni's mother turned down the radio, her long brown fingers with silver-painted nails tapping the dashboard for a moment. Then she said, "Eboni's been telling me about some mean old girls in your class. Sharron, let me tell you what I tell Eboni. Just because somebody has money doesn't mean they have heart or brains. It just means they have money. Okay?"

Sharron nodded again.

"Remember in *The Wizard of Oz*, when the Scarecrow was looking for brains and the Tin Man was wanting a heart? Remember what the Lion needed?"

"Courage."

"Well, you gotta have courage to stand up to these girls. 'Cause Lord knows they must not have much heart or brains to do what they did. Two of them, right?"

"Piper and Paige."

Eboni's mother nodded and turned her car toward the market. "Sounds like a bad fairy tale." In the parking lot, she turned Sharron's face to her with her long fingers. "Eboni told me about your daddy, too. That you think you'll never see him again. But you know what? You might. He might come back. Eboni's daddy is gone forever. We only have pictures. And memories. But Eboni had to get stronger because of that. She and I are a team."

"And Freckles the rabbit."

Eboni's mother smiled. "And you and your mama have each other, and The Friskative Dog. That's his name, right?"

They went inside the store, and Sharron's

mother opened her mouth so wide Sharron could see her silver tooth way in the back.

"You found him!"

She closed her register, because Leila waved at her to go outside, and they sat on the bench in front of the store. Sharron's mother held her and The Friskative Dog tightly.

"I'm Eboni's mother, Desirae. I saw Sharron here in need and gave her a ride. Someone found her dog."

"I'm Karen. Thank you so much for helping her."

Sharron told her mother about Nancy Cates and the trash can and the tag. Then she said, "And he smells like someone I know."

Eboni's mother said firmly, "Sharron, you need to talk to those two girls. And, Karen, you should probably talk to the teacher—she needs to know what's been going on. If you want, I can meet you at the school on my afternoon break. God don't like ugly, and I'm not a big fan of kids who have a whole lotta stuff and still aren't satisfied."

She got into her red Mustang, and the horse on

the hood winked silver when she turned around. Sharron said to The Friskative Dog, "We got rescued by a wild horse. And a nice mom."

Her own mother said, "You'd better tell me the rest of the story right now, Sharron. You walked to school? By yourself? Where did you meet Eboni's mother? Did you call Grandma Pat? She's probably frantic by now."

Then Sharron realized her mother was shaking. Her mother's earrings trembled. "I'm sorry, Mom. I just wanted my dog back so badly."

Her mother turned her face away for a minute, and Sharron knew her lips were trembling, too. Her mother didn't want to cry, not here. Her mother turned back and hugged her and said, "You can't ever take off like that again. Never. What would happen if you disappeared, too? Don't you understand how dangerous that was?"

She frowned and put her hands on Sharron's shoulders. "And you should never have taken your dog to school. I know you know that."

Sharron said, "I never will again." She put him in her backpack and left his head out, so he could see, while they walked inside the store. She imagined how dark it had been in the trash can, how there was no air, and she kept him on her back while they went into the office to call Grandma Pat. "Mom, can we help unpack cans from boxes and maybe sweep in the back?"

"I guess you'd better earn that allowance, since the tag saved your dog," her mother said, nodding.

When Grandma Pat came by an hour later, her hair was falling out of the tight white bun in little wispy tails around her neck, like she'd been running. She said, "I'm glad you found your doggie. I was busy all morning, and I have some more things to take care of this week, but on Saturday I'd like to come by and pick you both up for a special lunch." She put her hands up to her head, to work her hair back into the bun, and suddenly Sharron saw the way her father used to smooth his hair and put his hat back on. The hat that said SWIFT. Her grandmother smiled, and Sharron saw the one sharp tooth that was a little higher than the others. "My dog tooth," her father used to say, when she was little. "My left canine. Just like my mom's. That's how she could ID me if she had to. If I ever got lost, she said."

I don't have that tooth, she thought. I'm not going to get lost.

All afternoon, Sharron and The Friskative Dog stacked cans of tomato sauce on one shelf. Twenty. They stacked cans of refried beans on another shelf. Chili and tomato soup and tuna. Sharron tried to keep track in her head. One hundred cans. She ran her fingers through the bins of speckled pinto beans. Who could count those? No one. People bought them by the pound, in bags, and went home to add water and boil them until the beans would swell up and get soft and much bigger than when they were dry.

Sharron watched the clock. At two-fifteen, her mother said, "Sharron, this is the time for last period, right?" Then she said to Mrs. Reyes, "I'm going to Sharron's school now. I want to talk to the teacher."

Mrs. Reyes nodded and pulled a five-dollar bill out of the register. She held it out to Sharron and said, "Good work, *mija*. I like the way you stacked the tomato sauce."

But Sharron handed the money to her mother and said, "I don't need anything else now. I have my dog and his tag. My mom is the leader of the pack."

Mrs. Reyes and Leila laughed. Mrs. Reyes said, "That's smart, *mija*."

They walked in silence to the school. Sharron's mother held her hand, and in her other hand was the bag of today's groceries: apples, sausage, orange juice, and tortillas. "Scrambled egg burritos in the morning?" Sharron said finally, and her mother smiled.

"Are you scared? Your teacher won't be thrilled you brought your dog to school," her mother said.

Sharron saw Eboni's mother's red Mustang pull up to the curb in front of the school office. She said, "I'm not scared to tell the truth."

Her mother said, "Well, that looks like your class

heading out to the playground, right? Eboni's mom and I will go talk to Mrs. Monson, and you wait on the playground with The Friskative Dog."

She walked toward the classrooms, and Sharron walked onto the grass.

Everyone stared at her, and Eboni ran up to say, "You have him out of the backpack!"

Sharron said, "He got lost yesterday, and I thought he fell out during the fire drill, and I didn't come to school today because I was looking for him."

Brittany and Juan-Carlos and Ray came over, too, from the basketball court, and Ray said, "I remember your dog."

Sharron looked at Piper and Paige, who stayed over by the picnic tables. They stared back at her.

Courage, Sharron thought.

She said loudly to the group around her, "It was a mystery, what happened to my dog. But I found him." She walked toward the picnic tables, and Piper and Paige stood up and folded their arms.

Courage. Her friends were all around her. Sharron

said, "You two saw my dog when I had him at school. And you went back into the classroom to get the ball for PE. He was gone all night, and a lady found him in the trash two doors down from your house, Piper. He smells like that lotion Paige gave you."

Piper smiled and held her ponytail in her hands, tying her ribbon tighter. "So?"

Sharron said, "You called my dog pathetic. You always try to make me feel bad. Ever since first grade. But I would never hurt your dog, Carlotta."

Piper wouldn't look at Sharron. She looked at the other kids.

Eboni said, "I heard you guys laughing today about the dish towel that was the guide-dog jacket. Paige said her mother wouldn't even use that old dish towel to clean the floor."

Sharron breathed in hard. She said, "I rescued my dog. And I want my leash back."

Piper still wouldn't look at her. She looked at Ray.

Ray said, "Dang, you stole The Friskative Dog?"

Juan-Carlos said, "You could get suspended for stealing."

Piper shouted now, "She could get in trouble for having him at school! You're not supposed to bring toys to school!" She was pointing at Sharron. Her face was red, and her lips curled up like two fighting caterpillars.

"He's not a toy," Eboni said.

Sharron shouted back at Piper, "I know I shouldn't have had my dog at school. But that doesn't mean you can take him. Or make fun of him. Every time I say something in class, you try to make me feel bad. I don't feel bad, Piper! I don't want to be you! I want to be me. With my mom and my dog."

Then Sharron saw Mrs. G, the first-grade teacher, coming toward them. She must have yard duty for recess.

Mrs. G said, "What's going on here? Sharron, is that The Friskative Dog I remember from show-and-tell? What's he doing here?"

Sharron said, "He was lost, and I just found him."

Mrs. G raised her eyebrows. "On the playground?"

"No, someone stole him and put him in a trash can. Someone who won't admit it."

They all looked at Piper and Paige, and Mrs. G said, "Is this true?"

Paige suddenly raised her hand, as if they were in class, and Eboni rolled her eyes. Paige said, "I didn't do anything! Piper took the dog out of Sharron's backpack when we went to get the kickball. She hid him in her backpack and took him home with us. Then she made fun of him and dragged him around on his leash and stuck him in her closet."

Mrs. G folded her arms and said, "Paige, where were you when all this went on?"

They all stared at her, and Eboni said, "My mama says when you see something wrong and you don't stop it, you're just as guilty."

Sharron held her dog tight and said, "All of us are the same animals. My dad used to say that to me.

We have eyes and ears and mouths. Teeth. He said some animals are kind and some are vicious. And I learned that puppies start out the same, and how they're trained makes them into pet dogs or guide dogs. Good dogs or bad dogs." She felt her dog's eyes against her neck. "You try to make me feel bad because I live in an apartment and I don't have what you have. But I think you have bad training. I feel sorry for you."

Mrs. G said, "We need to sort this out with your teacher, girls. I see two moms and Mrs. Monson coming right now."

The adults were making their way through crowds of children playing basketball and tetherball.

Sharron saw her mother twirling around her wedding ring over and over while they walked. She saw her mother's earrings glint in the sun.

Paige started to cry very loudly.

Sharron said to Piper, "I want my leash back."

Piper looked right into her eyes this time. "I

don't have it." She put her hands out, palms up, like rain would fall into her fingers, and curled her lips again.

Juan-Carlos said, "I remember that leash from show-and-tell. It was purple."

Eboni said, "You have so much stuff and you stole her leash, Piper? That's pathetic."

Eboni's mother stood behind her now, and Sharron felt her own mother's fingers on her shoulder. Eboni said, "My mama says at the hospital, every mother and every baby are the same."

Her mother said, "That's right. We take care of you, and you, and you, and you." She pointed to each girl, with her long silver fingernails like flower petals. "That's how it's supposed to be."

But Sharron knew Piper didn't believe that, even though Paige was sobbing louder now and said, "I'm sorry! I'm sorry!"

"I want my leash back," Sharron said again, stepping toward Piper.

Then Mrs. Monson said, "Piper and Paige, your

mothers will both be getting letters from me about the meeting we will all have with Principal Jameson on Monday. Your behavior is inexcusable, from what I understand about this incident. Sharron did something wrong when she brought her dog to school, even though that was minor. If I had seen her dog, I would have told her not to bring him to class. But it sounds like Piper and Paige did something far more serious. I think your mothers will be truly disappointed."

Sharron's mother put both hands on Sharron's shoulders, and she felt her mother's breath light on her hair. Her mother said, "I'm proud of Sharron for being proud of her dog. She loves him. Not everybody gets to feel that kind of love. Not everybody's got heart like she does."

Eboni's mother said, "Or courage. Takes a lot of courage to love. But some people just have a lot of dog poop. In a lot of bags." She smiled at Piper. "I'm proud of Eboni for being a good friend." She lifted her finger toward Piper and Paige and said,

"Seems like some people need better lotion. Instead of Moonlit Path, they should be rubbing on some Get Over Myself."

"That would smell good," Sharron's mother said.

Sharron took her mother's hand and followed Eboni's braids toward the edge of the playground and then to the sidewalk. She was shaking inside, as if soda bubbles were inside her blood, but when her mother hugged her, the bubbles burst and everything was quiet.

Eleven

●●●●●●●●

You could count the bubbles on the pancake if you were quick, Sharron thought, watching her mother wait for them to burst before she turned the pancakes over. Fourteen. Wait. Then her mother slid the spatula under the yellow circle and turned it to the brown side, and no bubbles—just smoothness.

You couldn't count syrup. It disappeared into the pancakes. How did it taste exactly like it looked? Gold and shiny and melted.

Sharron sat on the couch with her dog. It was Saturday morning. She had washed him with his shampoo, and though his neck had frayed even more, and his back was showing his stitched spine in places, he smelled like himself now. Not like Piper.

She hadn't hurt him. She hadn't hurt his feelings. His eyes were brown and maple and gold on Sharron.

She didn't hurt my feelings, either, Sharron thought. She can't estimate anything. Not the number of palm fronds along the street, not the number of bees in the bottlebrush tree next door, not the number of tortillas in a truck.

One time, I estimated the recliners in a SWIFT truck, she thought. Eighteen.

She watched the mailman slide letters into the slots of the mailboxes. He slid envelopes into number 14.

Her mother was washing the dishes and then wiping off the stove. The burners were like black stars in the morning, but they were blue crowns of flame in the dark of Wednesday night, when her mother made coffee and Sharron had taken one spoonful in hot milk. They'd sat at the table for a long time. They didn't say to each other the words they'd said on the playground, but they were each hearing them again, Sharron knew. We are a pack of two, she'd thought. I have heart. You can't buy a good heart.

In the silence last night, Sharron had heard the first clickets, scraping their legs together outside the window in the hedges below. Her father used to say to her, "You hear those bugs singing to each other?" When Sharron was little, she used to say, "The clickets? I hear them."

She still had her father's words, in her head with her mother's.

She watched her mother pat her dog's head absently when she passed by the table. Now we're a pack of three again, she thought. She said to her mother, "The Friskative Dog and I will get the mail!"

She loved to put the key in the box.

Bills from the electric company and the gas company and the phone company. Her father had always hated the bills when he brought in the mail. All those numbers every month. Rent and food and gas for the stove and water for the sink and electricity for the lights. Her mother had always told her to turn off the faucet and turn off the lights. Her father used to say, "My money floats down to the ocean and flies off into the night."

My money.

Papers with President faces. Her mother counting it at the table at night. Papers and licenses and registrations.

She put the envelopes on the table and said, "When's Grandma Pat coming?"

"About an hour," her mother called.

Sharron sat at the table with The Friskative Dog and wrote a birth certificate for him on a piece of white paper. She decorated the edges first with scrolls of blue and black and then wrote lines, which she filled in: *Date of Birth: Christmas 2000. Place of Birth: Rio Seco, California. Owner: Sharron Baker. Breed: Labrador Retriever.*

Her mother picked up the envelopes and sighed. Then she sucked in air over her teeth, and Sharron said, "What?"

Her mother held a thin envelope. "This is his writing."

She opened the letter and read it silently. She put a piece of paper on the table. A money order for five hundred dollars.

Sharron saw the small blue letters backward through the thin paper her mother held. Six sentences. She saw a coyote loping down the street, all alone, staring straight ahead as his paws touched the white line in the middle of the asphalt.

Courage. Sharron said, "Is it from Atlanta?"

Her mother looked up, her mouth open. Then the edges of her teeth touched her lip. She said, "You heard your grandma and me that day."

Sharron nodded. "I'm not a baby anymore. You can tell me the truth."

Her mother finally said, "He's in Ohio. He left Atlanta. He says he was scared and he made a mistake and he shouldn't have thought so much about money. He says he's just going to drive now and do some thinking." She sat down in the chair and looked out the window at the street and the waving palm trees. "He says he's driving a few loads for another company in Ohio and he'll see where that takes him." She looked at Sharron now. "He says it might take him back here."

Grandma Pat's white biscuit bun bobbed into the window when she put down the bags she carried so she could knock, and Sharron flew to open the door before the knuckles could tap on the wood.

"A letter!" she shouted to her grandmother. "From Daddy!"

Sharron's mother and Grandma Pat read the letter again. Then Grandma Pat said, "He never did like writing long reports. Well, that's a lot for him to say, isn't it? He might end up here. Well. Well." She tapped the bobby pins in her bun, and the tiny clicks of her fingernails on the metal were like crickets inside her hair. "Well. That makes our lunch even more interesting. Come on."

She drove them only six blocks and turned down a narrow street lined with wooden houses, all with porches and front yards with roses and lemon trees and climbing vines on fences. Old houses. "Verbena Street?" Sharron's mother said. "I know that name. It's on Mrs. Rumer's checks."

Grandma Pat smiled. "Yup. She told me one day at the store what a nice street it was. So I thought I'd come see for myself."

She pulled into a driveway, and Mrs. Rumer herself was on the porch of a blue house with shingles and a steep roof and a lemon tree by the garage.

Sharron leapt out and said, "This is your house! Where's Curly?"

Mrs. Rumer waved and said, "Curly's at my house. Down the street."

Sharron's mother said, "Whose place is this?"

Grandma Pat said, "Maybe ours, if you want it. I think Sharron and her dog need a yard."

"A dog!" Sharron shouted. "You got me a dog!"

Grandma Pat held up her hands and said, "Don't get angry, Karen, I didn't get a dog. I just got a yard. That's all."

Mrs. Rumer came down from the porch and said, "Can I hold your dog for a minute? Where's his leash?"

Sharron told her quickly about Piper, and Mrs. Rumer said, "That girl is lucky The Friskative Dog didn't nip at her, a stranger like that trying to boss him around. Boy, I tell you. Some people are hard to train."

Sharron's mother was peering inside the front window at the living room. Sharron stood next to her, put her hands around her eyes like a swim mask, and saw an empty room with a fireplace and a wood floor.

Grandma Pat said, "Mrs. Rumer told me about this house for rent. I was thinking that maybe it's time for me to sell the old mobile home, since I'm getting tired of that gravel yard of mine. I was thinking this house has three bedrooms, and maybe we should pool our money together and move in. The owner says if we rented for a year, he might be willing to sell the place then. If we liked it."

"I like it!" Sharron yelled, running around to the backyard. The grass was tall and wet against her legs. She saw an arbor with climbing vines and a wooden fence at the end of the long narrow yard. When she turned around, she saw the back door, a cement patio, and, under an old tree, a doghouse.

"A bigger dog can't always sleep in the bed with his owner," Mrs. Rumer said from behind her. "A guide dog sleeps inside, but you never know when a doghouse might come in handy."

Grandma Pat came through the back gate, and Sharron ran to her grandmother and hugged her. "But do we have enough money, Mom?" she said, and then she saw her mother's face and remembered the letter.

Before her mother could speak, her grandmother said, "The rent is more than your place, Karen. But I can help, and Mrs. Rumer wants to offer Sharron an interesting proposition."

Mrs. Rumer said, "I love training guide dogs like Curly, but after all these years, I am a little tired of poop. So Sharron could clean up after Curly, if she wanted, and help groom him and do some other chores, and I'd pay her ten dollars a week."

Sharron said, "I can help with the rent!"

But her mother left the backyard. Sharron followed her as she walked around to the front porch and sat down on the steps. She stared out into the street. Verbena Street.

When the others came to the front yard, Sharron's mother said, "Mrs. Rumer, I'm so glad you're a friend of our family. But I need to talk to Sharron and my mother-in-law."

Mrs. Rumer handed The Friskative Dog back to Sharron and nodded. She said, "And I'm glad you're willing to have a friend. Sometimes people don't trust anyone who isn't related to them. I'm glad to have friends here, too."

Sharron threw her arms around Mrs. Rumer's waist, and Mrs. Rumer's belt smelled like Curly's favorite dog biscuits. Then she went back to the porch and sat on the step beside her mother's knee.

Her mother pulled the letter and the money order from her purse and laid them on the cement porch. She said, "Somehow I was afraid if I left this on the table it would disappear. I don't know why I'm carrying it around."

The sun came through the bars of the wooden railing and made gold stripes on the paper. Her father's writing was like a parade of blue spiders along the white paper when Sharron's eyes filled with tears. What if her mother said she didn't want the house, because they had to wait in the apartment for her father? For when he came home? For if he came home?

What if he never came home, and they waited forever?

Grandma Pat said, "Mother-in-law. Those are three funny words, Sharron. I became your mother's mother on paper. In law. When they signed that marriage license, I became her family. Just like that. My blood is in you through your father. But your mother and I share no blood. Just paper. And *you*. That makes love."

Sharron's mother pulled at the heart earrings, and they made the soft parts of her ears tremble. She said finally, "I know we're a family, with or without paper. Maybe we're a pack, too, like Sharron says. And in this pack, there're plenty of mom dogs who help out." She turned to Sharron and said, "I like this house. I like the yard. It will be a stretch for us— money will be tight."

"Could we afford dog food?" Sharron asked.

"Yes. I think it's time for another real dog," her mother said, petting The Friskative Dog on the head. "One more dog, to hang out with this one and add to our pack."

146

"Daddy always wanted a puppy," Sharron said.

"But moving here doesn't mean I'm giving up on your father. Neither should you."

"What if he comes to the apartment while we're here?"

Her mother wrapped a piece of the climbing vine around her finger like a green ring. "There's no address to write to on this envelope. But we can leave our new address with the post office and the apartment manager. When your father comes back, he'll find us."

"On Verbena Street," Sharron breathed.

"He's good at directions," Grandma Pat said. "Always has been."

"Math, too," Sharron said.

"Verbena Street's only six blocks away," Grandma Pat said. "Looks like this letter means maybe his amnesia's better. And his insomnia is keeping him thinking about us while he's driving. All those freeways. He loves the road."

Sharron's mom said, "Let's go look at the garage," and she and Grandma Pat went down the long driveway.

Sharron stayed on the porch. She looked out at the street past the front lawn, at the rosebush near the driveway. An old black mailbox leaned near the sidewalk, with numbers on the side: 4144. Coyotes could see anything, with their vision, when they loped down the center of a road. Her father had gotten lost, in Atlanta and Ohio, on the freeways, sleeping in his truck, dreaming of something else for a time. She thought about the orange blossoms he would never smell anywhere else, and the clickets he could hear only with her, and the handburgers he would eat alone in a diner while he thought of their kitchen table. He would come back. His love was not in slivereens, or he wouldn't have written the letter.

Sharron bent over her dog where he lay in her lap looking out at the street, too. She laid her cheek on his neck, his frayed soft worn fur nearly as smooth

148

as skin. As her own skin, pressed to his. "We have a porch, and a fireplace. In the winter, when we get wet outside in the yard, we can lay by the fire to get warm," she said. Then she whispered, "I'll never lose you again," her lips near his maple-brown eyes, and her breath made his eyes warm and wet as if he had tears that wouldn't fall.